"Jay, please,
I can explain…"

"There's nothing *to* explain," he told
her harshly. "Nadia is right. You're just
so jealous of her and so insecure that
you had to steal her identity."

"*I* was the one you held in your arms,"
Vanessa told him in a tortured tone.

"Yes, but only because I thought you
were Nadia. She was the one I wanted,
not you. Now that I've seen you
together, I think I must have been
blind," he said with deliberate
cruelty. "You're very much a pale
imitation of the real thing."

Vanessa begged him with her eyes to
understand, to let her explain, but all
he said was, "Nadia, if you're ready to
leave…."

Nadia turned to him, purring. "Once
you've known the *real* thing, darling,
you aren't likely to confuse me with
Vanessa ever again."

Books by Penny Jordan

These books may be available at your local bookseller.

Don't miss any of our special offers. Write to us at the following address for information on our newest releases.

Harlequin Reader Service
P.O. Box 52040, Phoenix, AZ 85072-2040
Canadian address: P.O. Box 2800, Postal Station A,
5170 Yonge St., Willowdale, Ont. M2N 5T5

PENNY JORDAN

rules of the game

Harlequin Books

TORONTO • NEW YORK • LONDON
AMSTERDAM • PARIS • SYDNEY • HAMBURG
STOCKHOLM • ATHENS • TOKYO • MILAN

Harlequin Presents first edition January 1985
ISBN 0-373-10755-2

Original hardcover edition published in 1984
by Mills & Boon Limited

CHAPTER ONE

'I AM sorry about having to leave you in the lurch like this Van, but I really don't have any option.' A winning smile accompanied Gavin's apologetic statement, and Vanessa quelled her urgent desire to tell her brother that 'leaving her in the lurch' as he put it, was one of the things he seemed to have a remarkable aptitude for. Even though she was the younger by two years, since the death of their parents, Vanessa had always felt a sense of responsibility towards her brother. 'You know the sort of shots we want, don't you,' he called, as he opened the studio door, 'the model's already been told.' He grinned at his sister, wicked amusement dancing in his deep blue eyes. 'You can always close your eyes!'

Vanessa groaned as the door closed behind him. At times Gavin really was impossible. By rights she ought to have refused outright to help him out today, but then he had worked so hard getting the studio going, canvassing for work and building up his reputation until he was the most sought after photographer in Clarewell, but to expect her to do the photographs for this advertisement he was booked to do, simply so that he could go and hero-worship a 'local boy made good' who had recently returned to Clarewell!

Stifling her irritation she busied herself in the studio, checking the carefully arranged background 'scene', and pulling a slight face. When Gavin had persuaded the town's largest employer to allow him to do the photography for their latest national advertising campaign they had agreed, but had stipulated a very small budget. Hardferns like many other companies were struggling to keep their lead on their competition, pruning down all extraneous costs, hence the 'background' depicting a lush tropical scene, instead of the real thing. Their new product was a revolutionary range of men's toilet products, including a skin-care range, and as Gavin had told her, Hardferns were very anxious to promote their new range with a tough macho image.

It was Hardferns publicity department who had suggested using a virtually nude male model while stipulating that the advertisements had to be in the 'best possible taste'. But it was Gavin who had dropped on her the bombshell that she was to be the photographer, and just so that he could go to the 'Welcome Home' celebrations at the town hall to laud the arrival of Jay Courtland, local football hero turned entrepreneur, who had astounded the press recently with his announcement that he intended to return to his home town and sponsor the ailing football team which had been responsible for his ultimate rise to fame as an England player. Now, at thirty-four, Jay Courtland had long since left the game—at least on the field, but rumour had it that he used the tactics he had developed there to assure him of a winning passage through the boardrooms he had conquered on his journey up the financial ladder. Was she the only person not to be impressed by his outwardly philanthropic gesture, Vanessa wondered sourly. Surely there were others who had drawn a parallel line between Jay Courtland's desire to promote his fourth division home team higher in the league, and the ailing sportswear company which was the latest of his many acquisitions. Who could tell, with Jay Courtland's support Clarewell might even make it as far as the Cup Final!

Suppressing her acid thoughts she freely acknowledged that they were partially motivated by Gavin's desertion. He was the one who was supposed to be in charge of this morning's session, and he knew how much she would dislike it. Her full lips pressed tightly together as she remembered the wicked amusement dancing in her brother's eyes. 'Twenty-two, and still a virgin!' he had mocked her on her last birthday, and although she had wanted to deny his teasing assumption they had both known that she could not. That was the trouble about living in such a small town. Everyone knew everyone else's business.

She glanced towards the back of the studio, frowning as her eye was caught by the portraits hanging there. They all featured the same woman. Hair like black silk hung water-straight down past her nude shoulders, her skin possessing the soft gleam of mother of pearl. Eyes the colour and depth of gentians shone out of a perfectly oval face, her nose and lips delicately carved, nostrils curled in a way that was faintly arrogant. It was a face that was intensely beautiful, holding both sensual allure and aloofness. It was in many ways the same face that Vanessa saw each morning when she glanced into her mirror, combing her

dark hair back off her face, securing it into the
confining clasp that kept it out of the way as she
worked. But her face was all that she had in
common with the girl in those portraits, she
thought grimly.

As children they had been inseparable. They
were the same age, she and Nadia. Their fathers
had been twins which was why they were so very
alike; alike enough for those who did not know
them to be confused, but the likeness was only
superficial. For as long as she could remember, she
had been the tomboy while Nadia had been the
pretty-pretty one; the one the adults always fussed
and cooed over. Even her own brother had not
been immune.

She sighed, as she worked steadily setting up the
equipment she would need. When their parents
had been killed in a climbing accident, she and
Gavin had turned quite naturally to their aunt and
uncle, sharing a common loss. Gavin had just
started up on his own then, and it had been Nadia
who had persuaded him to take the photographs
of her which she later submitted to the beauty
competition which had changed all their lives.
With hindsight Vanessa supposed they ought to
have guessed that Nadia would win. Although
physically their faces were the same, Vanessa had
always felt like a shadow standing next to the sun
when she was with Nadia. Nadia glittered and
drew people into her orbit like a flame attracting
helpless moths but unlike the flame she had no
warmth to give her victims. She used them to fuel
her own mammoth self-conceit, used them and
discarded them, as she had discarded Gavin once

she had accepted the modelling contract he had helped her to obtain. That Gavin had once loved Nadia Vanessa did not doubt, but her brother was not a child. He knew what their cousin was and what she wasn't.

Vanessa sighed, brushing grubby hands along her jeans. Tight and faded, together with one of Gavin's discarded shirts they were her normal working uniform. She rarely wore skirts or dresses, hardly ever used make-up, and did everything she could to minimise the similarities between Nadia and herself. Her refusal to do what Gavin called 'making the most of herself' annoyed him, she knew. He had often asked her to model for him but she always refused. On her eighteenth birthday he had given her a dress, a misty confection of silk chiffon in shades of blue to complement and match her eyes, and she had thrown it back at him in a fit of fury. 'You bought this for Nadia, not for me,' she had accused him, and they had quarrelled angrily about it.

'Why don't you admit that where Nadia is concerned you're suffering from one hell of an inferiority complex?' he had accused. She had denied it vehemently, but some part of her had recognised the truth. All her life she had been compared to Nadia, to her own discredit, much as her father had been compared to his older, and more forceful twin; and in an effort to fight against being dubbed 'second best' she had set out to make sure she was never, ever, taken for a poor carbon copy of Nadia.

Now they rarely saw her. She lived in London and her parents had retired to Bournemouth. She

paid Vanessa and Gavin brief visits occasionally,
always reducing Gavin to bitter invective, her
smug smile when he hurled his acid barbs at her
making Vanessa suspect that she enjoyed angering
him, knowing as they all did that he was simply
using his anger to mask his love and his pain.
Gavin had once in a rare moment of misery
confided to Vanessa that what hurt most was that
he himself had been responsible for setting her feet
on the path which had ultimately taken her away
from him. He had never said as much, but Vanessa
suspected that they had been lovers. It was hardly
a secret that Nadia enjoyed the company, and
caresses of the male sex. One only needed to open
a newspaper or a magazine. The last time she had
come home she had told them that she was hoping
to break into films.

'By doing what?' Gavin had asked harshly,
'Using the casting-couch route?'

Nadia had smiled sweetly at him, her long cat's
eyes slumbrous and mocking. 'If necessary,' she
had purred back, reminding Vanessa of a cat
toying with its prey, just waiting to pounce. Was
her cousin's well-publicised promiscuity the reason
she herself had remained so cold and withdrawn
with men? 'Frigid' was what more than one of her
dates had called her, and although she had
shrugged the slight aside her heart had ached,
because she had known that they had been using
her, wanting to possess her because they could not
possess Nadia, wanting her merely as a substitute
for her cousin, as she had been wanted all her life.

There were times when she wanted to tear
Nadia's portraits down from the studio walls. She

supposed most people would have described her emotion as jealousy, but there was more to it than that. She wasn't jealous of her cousin in so much as she wanted what Nadia had, she just wanted to be accepted for herself, not as Nadia's shadow. Many women she knew would have been delighted to look as she did; to look exactly like a famous model. But she hated the way she looked; hated her water-straight black silk hair, her perfect features, her sapphire eyes, because they were also Nadia's. Was her father going to be the only person who had noticed that her face had more character, that her eyes were warmer, her nature not shallow but generously giving?

What on earth had brought on that mood of introspection, she jeered, with self-mockery as she adjusted the silver umbrella reflector she was intending to use, before turning her attention to the spotlights so that they focused on the 'sandy beach', with the backdrop of soft supposedly South Pacific scenery and the deep blue of the water glimpsed enticingly through it. On the 'beach' prominently displayed were the products featured in the first of the 'ads'. A tanning lotion with a lot of heavy emphasis on its macho appeal in the advertising blurb. The caption for the ad. she was shooting today made Vanessa shudder. It was *All he needs to wear is Sunskin*, and if she hadn't known better she might have assumed that Gavin had deliberately set her up to take the session in his place.

Their father had been an explorer and both of them had learned about cameras and photography early. If her work was not quite as inspired as

Gavin's she did have an intuitive 'nose' for human interest work, and had sold several of her photographs to national dailies.

She glanced at her watch. Half an hour before the model was due. How would he feel when he realised that a woman would be behind the camera? All she could hope was that he was professional enough not to share her nervousness. Their budget was so slender that it would eat into their profit if Gavin had to re-schedule the session.

They had managed to keep on their parents' home on the edge of the town and Gavin had converted the cellars into his darkroom although he rented a studio in town.

She was just about to make herself a cup of coffee when she heard footsteps on the stairs leading up to the studio. Definitely masculine they caused tremors of apprehension to flutter along her spine. Not because she doubted her ability to do the job, but simply because . . . Because she was going to have to photograph a nude male! She made herself conclude the sentence. What was there to be so apprehensive about? The model was the one with the right to those feelings, not her. How Nadia would laugh at her if she could see her now. Vanessa glanced at her cousin's mocking portrait and smoothed sweat-damp palms over her shabby jeans, lifting her chin, unaware that the proud sparkle in her eyes made her look even more like the woman in the photograph, for once *her* features over-shadowed the made-up glamour of her cousin's.

The studio door was thrust open, and Vanessa tried to ease the dry tension in her throat. 'Hi!' she said casually, turning to fiddle with the spots so that she wouldn't have to face the newcomer and risk betraying her embarrassment. 'If you'll just strip off behind the screen.' She jerked her head in the direction of the tatty wooden screen in one corner of the room. 'I'll just finish getting ready here and then we can make a start.' He was earlier than Gavin had said, but at least that meant she wouldn't have to wait around getting steadily more nervous.

'I beg your pardon.' His voice was deep, edged with a harshness that made her spin round, her eyes widening as she took in the lean powerful length and breadth of his body. He was older than she had anticipated, somewhere in his thirties she guessed, and possessed of such an air of physical virility that she blinked dazedly as she studied him. This man was dynamite; so potently male that he could have sold ice to Eskimo women simply by looking at them the way he was looking at her now. Her fevered, desperately nervous glance was caught and impaled by eyes of tawny gold, mountain lion's eyes, ringed with yellow fire, pure amber when the light caught them, her own bemused image thrown back at her as she stared up at him. Tall herself, he towered over her, making her feel as fragile and vulnerable as a wind-flower in the eye of a storm.

Gradually she became aware that she was exhibiting all the classic symptoms normally associated with a massive teenage crush on some remote idol. Her heart was pumping at what felt like ten times its normal rate; her pulses racing in time. Her legs felt like the best quality feather down, and she knew, just knew, that it was only willpower that was holding a betraying blush at bay. And this was the man she was supposed to . . .

No! her mind shied away, and she wondered furiously if Gavin had known. For some reason she had visualised the model as blond and boyish, a beach-boy personified; not this dark-haired, golden-eyed predator whose face was as classically flawless in its way as her cousin's, and whose eyes moved automatically over her body, assessingly, insolently, she told herself angrily when his glance came to rest on the heaving thrust of her breasts.

'We're wasting valuable time,' she told him in a clipped voice trying not to betray her inner agitation. They were two professionals for heaven's sake, hired to do a job, and here she was, mooning over him like some crazed adolescent. 'The screen's over there,' she gestured to it again. 'I hope it's warm enough for you.' He was dressed in jeans and a cotton shirt, open at the throat, and she had to drag her eyes away from the tawny vee of flesh exposed. Gavin had turned up the heat before he left, saying impishly, 'we don't want our bronzed hero covered in goosebumps, do we?'

When he didn't move, Vanessa frowned. He was studying her with lazy insolence, tinged with curiosity as though she were something outside his normal experience. It couldn't be embarrassment that held him immobile. She doubted that she had ever seen any man less likely to suffer from embarrassment. Far from it. He probably got a kick from knowing that millions of women would be drooling over his naked form, she thought waspishly, trying to ignore the tiny voice that demanded to know how she knew they would drool.

When he didn't make a move Vanessa said crossly, trying to hide her nervous tension. 'You *are* aware that these shots are to be in the nude aren't you? Gavin did tell you?' She looked pointedly at the small set. 'I've put the stuff out already, we haven't got much time, so——'

Before she could protest he strolled over to the set and picked up the suntan cream, an amused smile curving his mouth. His bottom lip was full, and just for a moment she wondered what it would be like to feel its hard warmth against her own. She realised that while she had been daydreaming he must have said something because he had moved away from the 'set' and was studying the portraits on the wall. He glanced from them to her and said suavely, 'Quite a change. When did you decide you preferred being behind the camera to being in front of it? From these . . .' he tapped the portraits, 'I would have thought you had already found your forte.'

'Please hurry up and get undressed,' Vanessa snapped, too on edge to correct him and tell him that she wasn't Nadia.

'So impatient,' his golden glance mocked her, encompassing her flushed face, and the sparkling anger of her sapphire eyes, 'and so very flattering. Women are seldom so direct!' His eyes continued to mock her, and Vanessa had to clench her fingers into her palms to prevent herself from snapping a hostile retort. 'Okay,' he drawled when he saw her expression. 'I get the message.' He picked up a board carrying the slogan the company were using to launch the product and his eyebrows rose, laughter gleaming in the amber depths of his eyes, before he strolled across to the screen.

Vanessa busied herself checking her Nikon, steadily refusing to admit the increasing tension building up inside her, trying to blot out the brief rustling of clothes.

'Ready?' He walked towards her as nonchalantly as though he were still wearing his jeans and shirt instead of only ... With a tremendous effort of will Vanessa dragged her eyes away from his lithe body, telling herself she was a coward for being relieved that he had not dispensed with his clothing entirely, but had retained a pair of very brief briefs. His body was tanned and supple, his ribcage and stomach hard and flat. His body struck her as being that of an athlete rather than a man who spent hours in the gym building unflatteringly overdeveloped muscles. Rich colour stung her face as he drawled, 'Where exactly do you want me?' And she sensed that he was amused by her embarrassment. Stifling it, she pointed to the small 'beach' watching professionally as he sat down on it.

The set was designed for a reclining shot and she suppressed a sigh as she asked him stiltedly to move. She had worked with several male models but he was the most physically over-powering she had ever come into contact with—and the least professional ... He seemed to have little or no idea of what was expected of him, and when she complained for the third time about his pose, he said lazily, 'Well then you'd better come over here and show me exactly what you *do* want.'

The spotlights were hot, but they alone were not responsible for the prickles of perspiration she could feel breaking out on her skin as she directed his movements. At one point her breasts were on a level with his eyes and although her body was perfectly respectably concealed by the clothes she was wearing his glance seemed to strip that protection away, her face and body hot with colour as she tried to deny her physical response to his scrutiny. As he moved in obedience to her commands, his forearm brushed against her breasts. She stepped back instinctively almost overbalancing, forced to witness the amusement in his eyes—amusement which darkened to something else—something alien and half frightening as he witnessed her immediate rejection of their physical intimacy.

'Beautiful and clever,' he murmured softly, 'the dove fleeing from the hawk, not knowing that her very flight promotes his pursuit, unlike you, who I am sure knows very well what effect she has on the male sex.' Vanessa started to protest, the words stifled in her throat as he reached out carelessly and unbuttoned the top of Gavin's shirt exposing the pale curves of her breasts, one lean, brown finger tracing a lazy path down from where the pulse thudded at the base of her throat to the valley between her breasts. 'Your skin is so pale and soft, an enticement to any man to taste and touch it. Is that why you keep it this colour? Because you know that when a man looks at you, so pale and fragile, he can't help visualising your body beneath his own? Pale and beautiful like the moon, but not as cold one trusts?' There was amusement in his voice, as though the words he was saying to her were perfectly common-place.

'And you, I suppose, are the sun,' she snapped back at him, disturbed by the effect he was having on her, by the liberty he had taken without her doing a thing to stop him.

'Is that how you see me?' His teeth were white against the dark tan of his face, his eyes a shower of gold as he smiled at her.

'Very symbolic, don't you think?' Somehow he had moved and his fingers were at her nape, propelling her slowly towards him. 'I think of you as the moon, and you think of me as the sun. If those two planets were ever to come together, the effect would be cataclysmic, wouldn't you say?' His voice was light, but his eyes ... Vanessa shuddered as she read the message so explicitly portrayed in his eyes, and knew that he was already anticipating making love to her, and quite unashamedly letting her know it. This man is dangerous an inner voice warned her. Like the sun he will burn and destroy you if you get too close, and her skin as he had said was pale, far too pale for her to risk being scorched by any sun-god.

She jerked away from him, resisting the pressure of the fingers playing against her nape, and overbalancing. To support herself she flung out her hands, grasping the nearest solid object, recoiling when she realised it was his shoulder, his skin warm beneath her tense fingers, his body relaying a thousand differing and yet similar sensations to hers. So gradually that she was barely aware of it, her fingers uncoiled, their touch a gently feminine caress, her eyes registering her bemused and conflicting emotions. The brief, searing contact of a warm male mouth against the pulse beating so desperately at the base of her throat, made her jerk back, her eyes widening in dismay. He laughed, softly, deep in his throat.

'I am not Dracula you know, intent on stealing away your life blood, although I must admit when you look at me like that, like a frightened doe hearing the sounds of the hunter it does tempt me to . . .' He was tending his head to her throat again, and she was completely powerless to stop him Vanessa thought wildly.

The sudden, shrill ring of the telephone arrested them both, and Vanessa made good use of his momentary relaxation to slip away from him. The phone was in the back part of the studio, in the small room that Gavin used as his office. It was a call from someone enquiring about wedding photographs and by the time she had dealt with it Vanessa had managed to convince herself that she had imagined that frightening pull on her senses, that surge of feeling so intense that for one moment she had been in danger of drowning under it.

Forcing herself to appear calm she walked back into the studio and then came to an abrupt halt. There was no sign of the model! She walked over to the screen and glanced behind it. His clothes had gone too. Frowning she walked back to her camera, and then noticed the note propped up on it. *Just remembered I have to go somewhere—next time can I suggest I 'pose' somewhere more comfortable!* Dark colour surged into her face. She couldn't ignore the suspicion that he thought it had all been a game. Anger surged through her as she contemplated the implications of his note. What did he think she was? Some sort of ... of sexual deviant who enjoyed photographing nude men! She was so angry that her hands were trembling. She paced the studio furiously, rehearsing what she was going to say to Gavin when he returned. If this was his idea of a joke! If he had deliberately set this whole thing up! She knew her brother disapproved of her single state and of her life-style. She was missing out on life he had told her, but if he thought he was doing her a favour by introducing her to some ... some studio lothario ...

She was still seething ten minutes later when she heard Gavin's footsteps on the stairs, but the angry words tumbling on her lips were forgotten as he rushed in and she saw his harassed expression. 'I've missed him then?' he groaned, running irate fingers through his hair. 'Dear God that's all I need. How on earth am I going to persuade him to use us as the team's official photographers after this débâcle? What did he say, Van? Was he very angry? It's all the fault of that stupid girl at the town hall. She told me I had to be at the party, but according to his aide, he was coming here to meet me. He wanted me to do a shot of him for the local paper—you know they're doing an article on him. I suppose he was furious when he got here. They say he doesn't suffer fools gladly, and of course you wouldn't know why he was here.'

A cold, horrible feeling of disquietude was beginning to seep through her. At least it had started as a seep, now it was a fully fledged mill race. 'Gavin ... who exactly are you talking about?' she asked her brother.

He gave her a brief impatient frown. 'Jay Courtland of course. I told you I was supposed to be meeting him today at the Welcome Party, but apparently the arrangements had been changed and they hadn't let me know. He was to come here for me to do a formal picture of him for the paper.'

'What's he like, Jay Courtland?' Vanessa asked him hollowly, Please God don't let it be true, she was praying inwardly, but she knew her prayers weren't going to be answered when Gavin said impatiently, 'What do you mean what is he like? You must have seen photographs.' When she shook her head, he went into his office and she heard him rifling through some papers. Within seconds he re-appeared proferring a magazine to her. It was one of the Sunday Supplements and Jay Courtland's photograph occupied an entire page of glorious technicolor, right down to the amused amber eyes.

'*That*'s Jay Courtland?' She whispered it through stiff lips, still hardly able to comprehend.

'That's him, all right. Vanessa what's the matter? Did he come here?'

'He came, all right.' Vanessa told him, trying to hold back the hysterical bubble of laughter fighting for release. Jay Courtland; the local hero made good. The man who could be so important to Gavin's future, because Gavin hoped to impress him enough for Jay Courtland to use him on the

national advertising campaign for his new sportswear acquisition. If Gavin got that contract he
would be made, and it was well known that Jay
Courtland intended to favour local industry, local
firms. Only because it was good publicity Vanessa
had said scornfully when Gavin had talked about
it, and now . . .

'Van, what the devil is going on? What did you
say to him?'

'Oh nothing much,' Vanessa assured her brother
with false blitheness, 'I only asked him to strip off.
So that I could take his photograph you know . . .'

For a moment Gavin simply stared at her, and
then pulling himself together with a visible effort,
he shook his head and muttered, 'I don't think I'm
hearing this . . .'

'I thought he was the model,' Vanessa told him.
'I . . .'

'What happened? Why did he leave?'

'He went while I was on the phone,' Vanessa
told him.

'I hope to God he sees the funny side of this
Van.' Gavin looked very disturbed. 'He can make
or break us, you know that . . .'

'I don't suppose I'm the first woman to have
asked him to take his clothes off,' Vanessa
interrupted sardonically, but in truth she was
feeling far from as assured as she was trying to
appear.

'So that she could photograph him for a
suncream ad?' Gavin asked grimly. 'I'd better
phone his office—if they're still speaking to me.
What on earth made you think he was a model?'

She had been so tense, so nervous, so anxious to

get the whole thing over that she hadn't thought too deeply about it at all.

'God, a fine impression of our professionalism and skill you must have given him,' Gavin added, making her feel more guilty than ever. It had been bad enough when she had thought him a model, but now . . . her face burned when she remembered his outrageous comments; the warm, hard pressure of his mouth against her skin.

'He thought I was Nadia,' she told Gavin stupidly, shivering a little with reaction and shock. 'So I wasn't the only one to make a mistake.'

'Did you tell him you weren't?' Gavin was moving towards the office.

'No, there didn't seem much point.' If he had known that she wasn't Nadia, Nadia who the whole world knew loved a lover, would he have been as familiar with her?

She heard Gavin asking to speak to him, and not wanting to listen to his conversation, closed the office door and went downstairs intending to slip out and do some shopping, praying as she did so, that Jay Courtland would not punish her brother for her mistake.

Her mistake. For a second rebellion flared to life inside her, he had hardly done anything to correct it, but then perhaps he was so used to people recognising him that he had expected her to do so as well. Arrogant, lordly creature, if it was not for the fact that he held Gavin's future in the palm of his hand she would be tempted to wish that he would take offence. But Gavin could not afford to have such a powerful enemy. She remembered the way he had laughed at her when she tried to get him to pose, gritting her teeth as she re-lived the amusement glinting in his eyes. He had enjoyed being deliberately obtuse, she realised that now. If anyone should feel resentment it ought to be her, not him!

CHAPTER TWO

'I CAN'T get anything out of Russell Jackson, Jay's aide,' Gavin said fretfully when he rejoined her. 'He seems to be under the impression that the photo session has been delayed. Perhaps Jay hasn't told him what happened. I sincerely hope not, I dread to think what it will do for our reputation if it gets out that you confused Jay Courtland with a male model.'

'Is there such a vast difference?' She sounded more cynical than she intended and Gavin gave her an exasperated glare. 'Look Van, for some reason you seem to have a down on the poor guy and have done ever since we heard he was coming back, but even you have to admit he's done pretty well for himself. From living in an orphanage to becoming close to a multi-millionaire in thirty-four years is pretty good going.'

'That depends on how you assess progress,' Vanessa told him waspishly, 'there are more things to life than playing football and making money.'

'Come on Van, you're being unreasonably prejudiced. Look at his business record; the money he's given to charity.'

'And the publicity he's got for it,' Vanessa reminded her brother refusing to be swayed. 'You're entitled to your opinion Gavin and I'm entitled to mine.'

'I wish to God I knew how he is reacting to this morning.' He glanced at his sister.

'Well unless he gets in touch with us we're not likely to find out are we?'

'We could.' His glance held hers. 'If you went to see him and . . .'

She had known her brother too long not to guess what he was going to say. Her stomach seemed to drop away leaving shock mingling with her anger. 'And what? Apologise?'

'Explain,' Gavin palliated. 'We owe him that at least . . . Come on Van,' he protested when he saw her truculent expression. 'You must admit that.'

'Gavin I . . .'

'Look it's our whole future I'm talking about here Van. You know how much it costs to run the house; the rates alone . . . If I can't make a go of the studio . . .'

He frowned and for a moment looked so tired and drawn that her conscience smote her. By his lights Gavin undoubtedly had a case. After all he hadn't met Jay Courtland and been subject to his virile mockery; his subtly sexual onslaught against her senses. No doubt Gavin was looking at the whole matter in the light of the damage it could do them professionally whilst she . . . She bit her lip frowning. She didn't want to submit to the humiliation of apologising to a man who she knew would enjoy receiving her apology, who she suspected had believed she had deliberately . . . A fresh thought struck her. Could Jay Courtland have thought that she *knew* his real identity all the time? Dark colour burned her pale skin. If that

was the case she had to admit her mistake if only
to convince him that it had been genuine.

Almost as though he had picked up on her train
of thought Gavin said perplexedly, 'What I can't
understand is how you could have mistaken Jay
for the model in the first place ... Surely you've
seen his photograph often enough recently to
recognise him? It's been plastered all over the local
rag and then there's all the advertising the football
team have been doing. It isn't every day that a
World Cup player returns to the fourth division
club he first started off with with the express
intention of giving them financial aid. In fact
there's many a first division club that would like
to be in Clarewell's position now. Bill Stoakes, the
manager, is over the moon.'

'Is he?' Vanessa asked acidly. 'Personally I'm
more concerned about all the local lads who are
going to find themselves dropped from the team
once Jay Courtland starts waving his cheque book
around.'

'What on earth gave you that idea?' Gavin shot
his sister an exasperated look. 'Why do I get the
impression that you've got a blind spot where Jay
Courtland's concerned? It can't be because you
harboured a youthful adoration for him—you
were never a football fan, so what is it?'

'Nothing,' Vanessa lied shortly. How could she
explain to her down to earth brother that
everything she had read in the national press about
Jay Courtland before he announced his return to
Clarewell irritated her? He was a rich tycoon, a
man who lived and played hard; who made no
secret of his orphanage upbringing; or the fact that

he had had to fight hard for all that he now owned. She had visualised him as something of a rough diamond; a man who carried his game-playing from the football field to the boardroom and who was worlds removed from the sort of man who would appeal to her. Her tastes ran to men who shared her love of music; the theatre and the other arts; men whose idea of enjoyment was a day spent at the National Gallery as opposed to Wembley Football Stadium; a man who did not make sport and being 'one of the boys' his Gods. In short, a man as far removed from Jay Courtland as it was possible to get. If she had to visualise a career for this mythical man it would be as a doctor, or a solicitor, something that demanded exercise of the intellect rather than the body. If she explained any of this to Gavin he would doubtless accuse her of being silly, even perhaps of being faintly snobbish, but there was nothing of this in her feelings, it was simply that men like Jay Courtland were not her type. She did not believe for one moment that his generosity to his home town was purely philanthropic. How could it be when one took into account his reputation?

'Look Van,' Gavin began with brotherly impatience. 'You've got it all wrong. Jay intends to keep the team a local one; in fact he's determined on that; he wants others to have the chance he had; the chance to use their skill on the football field to escape the near poverty he had to endure as a child. That's why he's financing the new sports and leisure complex; that's why he's reequipping the local team to such a high standard.'

'And of course his generosity has nothing to do

with Supersport, I suppose?' Vanessa asked sardonically. 'Honestly Gavin you must think I'm a real dunce.'

'I'm not denying that he will want to make Supersport as successful as all his other companies, but you can't use that to detract from what he is doing for the town. If you discount everything else there are still the jobs that Supersport will bring to the town when he expands it as he intends to do.'

'By fermenting a good deal of national public interest in his ex-local football team? By kitting out them and all other local would-be athletes for free?'

'Okay, so there is something in it for him, and he can be a hard man, but he's got reason to be Van. Abandoned by his mother when he was five years old; never knowing his real father, because his mother never married him and she died before he was old enough to talk to him about him; living in an institution . . . He got a place at university, he could have gone to Oxford you know, but he couldn't afford to support himself while he was there, even with his scholarship so——'

'He became a footballer instead, swopping graceful spires for the adulation of his fans? You're breaking my heart . . .'

'As you'll break mine, if I lose the promise of this contract. You will go and see him won't you Van?'

'Do I have much option?' she asked her brother dryly, adding, 'Yes I'll go, and if I were you I'd check up on the whereabouts of our real model.'

There was no point in putting off the evil hour unnecessarily. Gavin told her that Jay's aide had said he could be found at Supersport, but just as she opened the studio door Gavin yelled after her, 'Van, go home and get changed first. If you go dressed like that they'll never let you in the place . . .'

Suppressing an angry grimace Vanessa stepped out into the sunlit street, heading for the battered Volvo estate both she and Gavin shared.

It didn't take her long to drive to Clare Lodge, the home her parents had bought shortly after their marriage. Set in the rolling countryside of the Cheviots the lodge commanded almost idyllic views of the hills. The approach road was unmade up and pot holed, but the Volvo was too used to it to do more than protest mildly, unlike the expensive foreign make sportscar which she only narrowly managed to avoid as it came racing down the lane towards her. Only by swerving almost into the ditch was there room for its driver to get past, and Vanessa had a blurred impression of dark hair before her attention was concentrated on maintaining control of her own vehicle.

The lane led only to Clare Lodge and the Manor House beyond, and she frowned wondering if the driver of the other car had merely lost his way or had had a definite mission down the muddy narrow track. The Manor House had been up for sale for over twelve months and before that had fallen into decay, occupied only by General Adaire, an eccentric, ex-army man who lived there alone after the death of his wife.

More out of curiosity than anything else, Vanessa drove past the gates of the lodge and headed towards the Manor House proper coming to an abrupt stop as she saw the padlocked gate and the 'No trespassers' signs. Where the old, faded 'for sale' notice had hung a new notice now stood, a bold 'sold' sticker plastered across it. Someone had bought the Manor.

Musing on who it could be and hoping it would not, as had been rumoured at one time, be a property developer intent on turning what had once been a gracious country house into a multitude of small flatlets, Vanessa reversed down the lane to the lodge. As its name implied it had once been the lodge to the Manor House, but had been modernised and extended from its original Tudor framework during the Edwardian era, when it had been occupied by the mother of the then incumbent of the Manor. Having known no other home Vanessa was fiercely devoted to the lodge. How much longer would they be able to keep it though if Gavin did not get the contract he was hoping for from Supersport? Yet another reason for her to tender her apologies to Jay Courtland. Surely her love for her home outweighed her discomfort at the thought of facing the man who had mocked her so sardonically in her brother's studio?

Less than an hour later, showered and wearing a simple pale yellow linen suit she had bought on impulse in a boutique several weeks ago, she was driving the Volvo in through the gates of Supersport. She had visited the factory once before and as then she was struck by its general air of neglect and decay, hardly the image of a go-ahead competitive firm, she thought as she eyed the untidy loading bay and the rather decrepit vans waiting there.

The only space to park the Volvo was right next to ... Her heart missed a beat as she studied the unmistakable lines of the exotic sportscar she had last seen coming down the road from the Manor. A brief glance at the personalised numberplate told its own story and her face flamed as she remembered their brief contretemps in the lane; JAC 1, the numberplate read and she wondered idly what the 'A' stood for as she forced herself to breathe evenly and deeply, summoning all her courage and composure for the interview ahead.

As she locked the car and walked towards the reception area she heard voices gradually coming nearer, and recognised Jay Courtland's, much sharper and more authoritative than she remembered it. 'All deliveries will be tendered out— at least until we get the factory working reasonably efficiently.' Vanessa heard someone else objecting, but Jay Courtland cut ruthlessly through the objections announcing crisply that he had made up his mind and that he was not prepared to waste valuable time on discussing the matter further.

She had just reached the main door when the small party of men rounded the corner. There were five men altogether, Jay Courtland easily discernible; easily the most arresting, his lean, tall frame standing out from those of his fellows; tired-looking, business-suited individuals whom she recognised as the directors of the once family-run firm. Jay Courtland saw her first, and saying something to his companions left them to walk towards her.

'Ah ha, it's the lady who wants to photograph me in the nude,' he mocked her with a taunting smile. 'You're nothing if not persistent, but you can hardly expect me to strip to the buff here, or was it bribery you had in mind this time?' His glance rested provocatively on her breasts as he spoke, and the suit which had seemed eminently respectable and suitable when she put it on suddenly seemed to cling far too seductively to the curves of her body, the silk shirt she was wearing beneath it, far too revealing. Only pride and a certain grim determination not to let him rattle her prevented her from hugging the edges of her jacket protectively around her body, but as though he knew what was running through her mind Jay lifted his glance from her body to her flushed indignant face, laughter gleaming gold in his tawny eyes. 'You know I can't imagine you as a model somehow,' he said softly, 'You don't strike me as a young woman who would docilely allow herself to be ordered what to do. Something tells me you prefer being the one who does the ordering. Is that why you prefer being behind the camera to being in front of it?'

This was the moment to tell him that she wasn't Nadia, but just as she opened her mouth, the main doors opened and a slim, harassed looking man in his mid-forties hurried out, relief clearly evident in his expression as he saw Jay Courtland.

'Jay, there you are. There's a call for you about the new contracts we're hoping to set up for Supersport. Will you . . .'

'Tell them I'll ring back in fifteen minutes will

you Russell. I think this young lady has something
to say to me that just won't wait.'

Vanessa went scarlet as she felt the other man's
interested gaze skim over her, and then Jay was
taking her arm and guiding her in through the
open doors, down a carpeted corridor coming to
an abrupt halt outside the farthest door. Thrusting
it open he stood back so that Vanessa could
precede him inside. The room still smelled of fresh
paint and had obviously been re-decorated and re-
furnished. Her mouth twisted in a slightly bitter
smile. Of course everything would have to be
bright shiny new for the new owner.

As though he guessed what she was thinking Jay
Courtland watched her mobile face for a few
seconds before offering, 'Packaging my dear Nadia,
you of all people should know how important that
is. How can we hope to persuade our buyers that
Supersport's products are the best if we try to sell
them from grubby, tatty offices?'

'Spend money to make money?' Vanessa asked
acidly. 'I should have thought you already had
more than enough of that commodity?'

'A man can never have too much of any
commodity he prizes,' Jay told her sardonically,
'and I learned young the value of money; the
status and power it confers upon its owner.'

'And that's what you want? Status, power?'

'Is that so wrong?' He walked over to the row of
modern cabinets with their smoked glass fronts
and extracted a bottle and two crystal glasses. 'The
respect of our peers, isn't that what all of us want?'

'Respect can't be bought,' Vanessa told him
defiantly.

'You think not?' His mouth twisted wryly. 'You think the Mayor would still be wanting to dine with me if I was still Jay Courtland, bastard orphan of this parish? Would I be enjoying the company of a beautiful woman like you if I was still the same Jay Courtland I was at fifteen?' His eyes and mouth told her that he thought he knew the answer, and Vanessa realised for the first time how much bitterness there was concealed behind the mocking mask; the smooth urbanity with which he faced the world. How could she tell him that no matter what he had done in life he would always have been a man who commanded the attention of others, especially her own sex. He opened the bottle he had been holding in his hand, the popping of the cork alerting Vanessa to its contents. 'Veuve Cliquot,' he drawled as he poured the foaming clear liquid into the fluted champagne glasses. 'Your favourite I believe.'

Just about to correct him Vanessa realised that it *was* Nadia's favourite drink, at least according to the popular press. She wanted to tell him that he was mistaken and that she wasn't her glamorous cousin, but something more important took precedence. 'You bought that for me? But how did you know . . .'

'That you would come here?' He shrugged powerful shoulders and smiled. It wasn't a pleasant smile, Vanessa realised. Nor a warm smile, in fact it was cold and rather bitter, his eyes flat and empty as they studied her flushed face. 'Wasn't it part of the game that you should?' he asked softly, handing her one of the glasses. 'I must admit you showed ingenuity and since that is a trait I greatly admire, I felt it should be rewarded.'

Ingenuity? Vanessa stared at him, the truth suddenly so clear that it could have been illuminated in ten foot high letters outside the factory. She put down her glass so quickly that some of the frothy liquid spilled, anger darkening her eyes to deep sapphire as she faced him.

'I came here to apologise for this morning,' she said enunciating the words clearly and slowly so that there could be no mistake. 'I'm very sorry for what happened, but it was a genuine mistake. I had no idea. Everyone makes mistakes,' she added wildly, when it became plain that she wasn't getting through to him. 'Gavin did have a session booked.'

Jay had put down his glass and he came towards her, with a cool economy of movement that reminded her of a huge jungle cat. Even the way he walked possessed an undeniable sensuality she thought, watching him with one half of her brain while the other half struggled with the task of impressing upon him the truth.

When he reached for her hands she was so surprised that she made no move to evade him. 'I really can't allow you to call a halt now that the game has begun, it promises to be far too interesting. If it makes you feel any happier we'll forget about motives for the moment shall we and concentrate on this.'

'This' was the warm, firm pressure of his mouth on hers, as he parted her surprised lips with consummate ease, enfolding her in his arms almost before she even realised he had done so, and then once his mouth was in possession of hers, somehow it was impossible to pull away.

She had been kissed before of course. She could hardly have reached twenty-two and not had some experience with the opposite sex, but because of her inferiority complex she had always chosen as her dates boys and then men biased towards the intellectual rather than the physical, and the actual realisation of what a kiss could and should be totally overwhelmed her. Before she knew what she was doing she was holding on to Jay's hard shoulders, sliding her fingers into the thick silky hair at his nape, allowing him to taste and plunder her mouth as though she were no more than a ragdoll.

That he was the one to break the kiss was a humiliation she would dwell on more deeply when she was alone, for now it was all she could do to simply stand up, her eyes betraying her bedazzlement, while thick, dark lashes concealed his expression from her, his voice as warm and lazy as always as he commented softly, 'A most auspicious beginning, don't you think.' He reached out and ran his thumb along the bottom curve of her lip, watching the emotions chase one another through her dazed eyes, a tigerish smile springing to his mouth as he observed, 'For such a very experienced lady, you certainly have quite a few tricks up your sleeve, or did one of your lovers tell you how arousing that mixture of inexperience and enthusiasm can be?'

His words jerked her out of her bedazzlement and she pulled away, but it was too late to evade the hard pressure of his arms, and the even harder pressure of his mouth, as it reinforced his comments about her effect on him. This was no teasing, lazy kiss, but a man's expression of his powerful physical need and avowing his intention of appeasing it, in a very explicit manner. A pervasive indolence spread through her body, heating her blood, melting her resistance, every nerve ending concentrating on the feelings beating through her body. Her mouth opened of its own accord beneath the hard pressure of Jay's, her fingers sliding into his hair to prolong the caress, her body meltingly pliant against him so that she wasn't quite sure when she first felt the touch of his fingers against her breast, only that they seemed to burn through the thin silk of her blouse and she could think of nothing she wanted more than to be with him; to be part of him.

He tensed against her, lifting his head, and her body cried out its protest, her tongue touching her swollen lips. His eyes followed the brief movement. 'Someone's coming,' he told her huskily. 'You'd better go.' He bent his head, trailing his tongue tormentingly across the tender flesh she had just moistened, and when he lifted it again his eyes glowed as brilliantly gold as the sun. 'You do things to me I've only dreamed about,' he moaned against her throat. 'Think yourself lucky you got that phone call this morning, otherwise we'd have been making love on that damned "beach" of yours.'

She was at the door almost before she realised what was happening. When it opened Russell was there, looking worried and drawn. 'It's been more than fifteen minutes, Jay,' he complained, his thin face flushing slightly as he avoided looking at Vanessa. Had he guessed what had been happening? Did Jay make a habit of seducing every woman who walked into his life? Certainly according to the press there was no shortage of women willing to share his wealth with him. Sharp knives of pain raked over her skin, and for the first time she knew real jealousy. It was nothing like the feeling she had felt towards Nadia.

'Miss March is just leaving, Russell,' Jay assured his aide with a brief smile, and as she headed down the corridor to the main door, Vanessa had to suppress a faint shiver of reaction. In less than five minutes Jay Courtland had managed to turn her world upside down. Or had it happened before that? Even this morning, despite her resentment of him she hadn't been immune to him, and now, when he kissed her ... Her fingers touched her mouth and she trembled. Never had she experienced such a surge of physical desire; such an intensity of feeling that obliterated everything else until nothing mattered but the final, flaming consummation of that desire. Jay had wanted her too, he had told her so. Suddenly she seemed to have stepped into an unfamiliar world. The world she had inhabited before today didn't allow for such happenings, for ... falling in love! Falling in love, she was being ridiculous. Jay Courtland certainly hadn't fallen in love with her. Oh he wanted her all right ... She came to an abrupt halt suddenly remembering something else, a deep tide of mortification colouring her skin. He *didn't* want her, he wanted Nadia. He wanted the woman he had held in his arms and kissed, she told herself;

that woman was her. For the first time in her life she felt the urge to assert herself instead of creeping into the background. She was back at the studio before she remembered that she had not really apologised and nor had Jay shown any indication of accepting that the entire incident had been a genuine mistake.

Gavin greeted her with a wide grin. 'Guess who's just been on the phone?' he called out to her. 'Only Russell Jackson, Jay's aide. Jay's giving us the sole contract for photographing the new range when they bring it out, and he wants us to do the photographs for all the publicity the team will be getting. What do you think of that?'

'It's marvellous news Gavin.' He asked her about her interview with Jay, and she told him that it seemed to have gone well, hoping he would be too preoccupied with his own news to notice how few real details she was giving him. 'I've got another piece of news for you,' he told her. 'Jay's bought the old manor. Apparently he's tired of city living and he wants to settle down here. Shouldn't even be surprised if he decides to marry.' She had her face turned away from her brother so he couldn't have seen the sudden paling of her face, or noticed the ridiculous way in which her heart suddenly threatened to stop beating.

'To anyone in particular, or . . .'

'Oh, I'm just surmising, but surely he's going to want to pass on his wealth to someone? I've got to go and see him tomorrow, he wants to set up the publicity campaign for the team. I don't know how long it's going to take.'

She had been looking for a way of explaining to

Jay the mix-up over her identity and suddenly hit upon the ideal solution. 'Gavin, Jay still thinks I'm Nadia, will you explain to him tomorrow that I'm not. It's getting rather embarrassing.'

'If you want me to, although I can't see why you didn't tell him yourself today. Why didn't you?'

'I didn't really get the opportunity. I had to leave because he had a phone call to make.'

'Umm. Well while he was on he warned me that we can expect a considerable amount of activity up and down the lane for the next few weeks. The manor is practically derelict and he's getting an architect in to work on it, modernise it.'

Modernise it! Vanessa repressed a brief shudder. She could well imagine the results, a tasteless, brash amalgam of all that was modern and gimmicky. For the first time since she had left Jay's office reality impinged. They were two people who were worlds apart and until today his world was one she would never have dreamed of wanting to enter. She still didn't want to. But she did want Jay. The next move was up to him. Would he get in touch with her again once he knew who she really was, or was he too, having second thoughts? Had she only appealed to him as 'Nadia' March the famous model?

CHAPTER THREE

IT was Gavin who informed her of the exact nature of Jay's thoughts, when he returned from his meeting with him. They had no work on that day and Vanessa had elected to give the lodge a good cleaning. She had just finished and was sitting down with a cup of coffee when she heard the Volvo in the drive. Gavin got out looking elated, waving a thick bunch of papers.

'The contract,' he told her as she opened the door. He grimaced when he saw her coffee mug on the small table in the living room. 'I think we deserve to celebrate with something a little better than that.' He glanced at his watch and announced. 'I'm taking you out to lunch, go and put your glad rags on, and we'll go.'

Apart from her lemon suit there was little in her wardrobe to deserve the description 'glad rags', and in the end she selected a white cotton skirt and a pretty pastel toning tee shirt which had been a cast off from Nadia, who claimed that it was far too big for her.

Although both girls were slender, Nadia maintained an almost flat-chested model's proportions while Vanessa was more femininely curved, so that the tee shirt fitted snugly to her body.

As they drove through the countryside, now in full bright green June leaf, Vanessa recognised the route to what had been a favourite family haunt—

an old coaching inn which had been preserved and remained much as it must have appeared in Dickens' time.

Because it was mid-week they had no difficulty in getting a table, the landlord immediately recognising both of them. The inn specialised in local produce, Vanessa opted for a sea-food cocktail followed by steak, new potatoes and asparagus, both vegetables being grown locally. They had reached the main course before Gavin started to talk about his meeting with Jay Courtland. He waited for the wine waiter to move away and then started to tell her about the contract. 'It gives us the exclusive rights to do all the photographic work for Supersport, and all the publicity connected with the team. It's a relief to know that everything's tied up legally now,' he confided to Vanessa. 'Business has been too slack recently. I suppose London is really the place for a photographer to make a real success.'

'You've been doing very well,' Vanessa protested.

'Not as well as you think,' he told her ruefully. 'I haven't wanted to worry you by telling you how much we needed the money from this contract. I only found out after he died that Dad raised his share of the money for that last expedition by mortgaging the house. Unless we pay back a hefty sum this year, the bank could foreclose and we'd lose it.'

'As bad as that! You should have told me.'

'And have you worrying yourself to death about losing the lodge?' He shook his head. 'I must admit I was beginning to get desperate until I learned about the contract. And he was very nice about the mix-up yesterday. He seemed more amused than annoyed.'

'You did tell him that I wasn't Nadia, didn't you?'

There was a brief silence, and Gavin's expression changed, his face flushing slightly. 'You haven't told him have you?' Vanessa breathed. 'Oh Gavin . . .'

'Look I know I said I would, but the thing is, Van, he wants you to pose with the team; for a gimmick he said. He was so keen on it that I could hardly turn round and tell him the truth. Not when he'd just said that finding out you were my assistant was what had swung the deal our way. I couldn't tell him.'

Vanessa went pale, pushing her half empty plate away from her. 'But Gavin, that's dishonest. Letting him think I was Nadia . . .'

'Not really. It is *you* he wants to model with the team. After all he's seen you in the flesh and he hasn't seen Nadia.'

'But he thinks I *am* Nadia,' Vanessa protested, 'and the truth is bound to get out. The whole town knows who I am. Unless of course you're proposing deception on a grand scale.'

He had the grace to look slightly embarrassed. 'Look Van I know it places you in an awkward position, but what else could I do? There he was saying the contract was ours with one breath and then with the other suggesting that you wouldn't object to posing with the team as a publicity gimmick.'

'I can see that it was difficult for you, but surely

no more difficult than it's going to be when he finds out the truth?'

'Need he do?' Gavin fiddled awkwardly with his cutlery. 'Look Nadia's out of the country at the moment, I checked before we came out, a modelling job in Gambia and besides, she never comes back here. You know that.'

'Gavin you can't expect me to deliberately deceive someone; to pretend that I'm someone I'm not. Tell him the truth and if he still wants me to pose, then fine . . .'

'I don't see how I can now.' Gavin sounded truculent and Vanessa sighed. Her brother didn't want to admit to Jay Courtland that he had allowed him to believe she was Nadia, and she could understand that, but surely he could see how potentially dangerous it could be to deliberately allow him to go on under the same misconception. Apart from her own dislike of the thought of the deceit and subterfuge necessary to keep up the pretence.

'Van, I wouldn't ask if we didn't have so much at stake, believe me.'

'But Gavin, we can't go on deceiving him for ever.'

'No, I realise that. Once the photographs have been done and I've shown him the quality of our work, "Nadia" can disappear and "Van" can return. He might suspect the truth, but as long as we're discreet he isn't going to question it—he won't want to appear that foolish, and besides what harm will it do?'

How could she explain to her brother the delicacy of the situation between herself and Jay?

As far as she was concerned there was no
justification for deceiving him further, and now it
was too late, she cursed herself for not making her
identity plain earlier. But if she went to him now
and told him the truth it would be humiliating for
Gavin, and they could even lose the contract. She
was in a cleft stick, faced with Hobson's choice,
neither path appealing to her.

'Look Van,' Gavin pressed, sensing that she was
weakening. 'You only need to do it for a week or
so, no longer I promise you. You might even enjoy
it,' he added with a grin. 'Haven't you always
wanted to know how the other half live; what it's
like to be our glamorous, sought-after cousin?'

'Not at the price of my own integrity,' she
responded smartly, but inside she felt a tiny twinge
of despair. He desired her, Jay had told her, but
was it her he desired, or was it the woman he
thought she was? Was it the cachet of possessing
her cousin's famous face and body that drew him?
Would he still want her when he discovered she
was simply plain Vanessa? Second best all her life
and no competition at all for the glamorous
Nadia; a candle in comparison to the sun.

'I still don't think it's right, Gavin,' she told him
slowly.

'But you'll do it anyway? Steady, reliable Van,
always weighing the pros and cons ... Hurry up
and finish your meal,' he commanded her, 'we've
got a busy afternoon ahead.

'Busy?'

'Umm ... If you're going to be Nadia, you need
costuming for the part. The only jeans I've ever
seen her wearing are designer label. Jay was very

curious about why you were behind the camera instead of in front of it. I told him you had wanted a break and that you were helping me out.'

'Very inventive of you,' Vanessa said dryly, following her brother as he made to leave their table. He paid the bill and then they were out in the warm June sunshine; the first really warm day they had had and it seemed to be almost criminal to waste it on shopping, but Gavin was adamant. It was just as well he had such decided ideas on fashion because alone she could never have found the enthusiasm to buy the clothes he was pushing at her. She didn't even like touching them; silk dresses and blouses, fluid sensual clothes that conjured up a vivid impression of her clothes horse cousin. Clothes she would never have chosen in a million years.

'You know you look just as good as Nadia,' Gavin commented as he made her parade up and down in front of him, studying each outfit assessingly, 'in your own way. Where Nadia is sensual, you are innocent. In fact Jay remarked upon it, and said how surprised he'd been by the lack of sensuality which comes over so strongly in your photographs. He seemed to find it very intriguing. We'll have that one,' he added, picking out the bright pink taffeta dress with its low cut neckline that she had been wearing. 'And you'll need something really grand for the ball.'

'The ball?'

'Umm. He announced this morning that once the alterations on the house are finished he intends to give a ball there, proceeds from the sale of the tickets to go to the local children's home. It promises to be an extremely grand affair, but it's months away yet, you can get something for that later. You still need a dress for now.'

She tried on a selection of dresses half-heartedly, liking none of them until the assistant brought in the soft silk taffeta sheath. She tried it on in breathless anticipation marvelling at the apparent delicacy of her figure and the undeniable pleasure of wearing something so alluringly feminine.

When she showed it to Gavin at first she thought he didn't like it. The neckline revealed the smooth sweep of her shoulders and the rounded curves of her breasts, the narrow skirt outlining her hips. A very provocative dress she thought and she held her breath waiting for his comments, asking anxiously when he made none, 'What's the matter, is it too sexy, do you think?'

The smile he gave her was faintly crooked. 'It's not that, it's just that I've suddenly realised what we've all done to you, and what you would have been if there'd been no Nadia, and only a Vanessa. We'll take it,' he told the saleswoman.

An hour later they were back at the lodge. Because of the new contract Gavin had some work to do, and rather than sit brooding on the deception she was forced to be party to, Vanessa picked up her Nikon and wandered down into their back garden, finding the gap in the thick beech hedge which gave access to the Manor's overgrown wood. The wood had always been a favourite place of sanctuary during her childhood, a place where she could be alone to think and dream, and now she needed its solace once more. She had picked up her camera more out of habit more than anything else, but as she wandered along the overgrown bramble and nettle bordered paths she was glad that she had. Soon this small wilderness would be gone; this might be her last opportunity to record what had once been her secret place of refuge. Soon Jay Courtland and her false identity as Nadia were pushed to the back of her mind as she worked busily photographing the ancient oaks, the small, still pool where she had watched ducklings hatch; the stream where otters played and she had once seen a kingfisher. Gavin had once brought her here at night to watch the badgers, a truly magical experience; soon she was lost, wrapped in the dense silence of her surroundings transported from the materialistic and often alien world outside.

It was only when the angle of the sun started to drop sharply that she realised how late it was getting. Gavin would be wondering where she was. With a tiny sigh of regret she started to make her way back, coming to an abrupt halt as she heard someone moving towards her. All at once a primeval sense of fear swept through her an instinctive dread that made her regret her solitude. She shivered, on the point of plunging through the undergrowth when she heard Jay Courtland call out sharply, 'Who's there?' He rounded the bend in the path as he spoke, and a sharp sense of relief filled her.

'Nadia?' To say he sounded surprised was putting it mildly. It was the first time she had seen him looking anything less than composed.

'What a surprise. Were you looking for me?'

He was subtly reminding her that she was

trespassing. Vanessa guessed, suddenly conscious of her torn and grubby skirt and of the marks that were no doubt on her face and arms. Anything less like a glamorous model would surely be difficult to find!

'I'm sorry, I shouldn't be here,' she apologised, 'I heard you were having the Manor ... modernised, and I just wanted to take some photographs of the place as it was. I acted thoughtlessly, I should have asked permission.'

'Not at all.' He glanced from her Nikon to her grubby face and clothes. 'What exactly do you think I'm going to do to the place—tear it down and level everything to the ground?'

Her expression must have given her away, because his mouth tightened. 'I see—so I'm to be the complete philistine am I? The nouveau riche who equates cost with taste, is that it?'

'I'm sorry.' Somehow she stammered out the words, conscious of a great rage of anger bottled up inside him. 'It's just that I've always loved the wildness of this place . . .'

He was looking at her closely. 'Umm. Quite a bundle of contrasts, aren't you? I should have thought Kew Gardens or Hyde Park was more your idea of an idyllic country setting, not an untamed wilderness like this.'

'You're forgetting I grew up here.' She knew that she sounded stiff and defensive, but every time he reminded her that he thought she was Nadia she was consumed with guilt. It was never going to work. She was never going to be able to keep up the pretence.

'You've living with your cousin at the moment, I believe?'

Her face paled as she recognised yet another lie looming. 'Er yes . . . at the lodge. He tells me that you intend to hold a ball here when everything's finished.'

'Ah yes, I thought that was rather more your style.' Although he smiled there was far less warmth in his voice. 'Women do so enjoy showing off their fine feathers don't they, and by all accounts you've collected quite a nice array of jewellery from your admirers.'

Vanessa felt sick as she realised the article he must be referring to. It had been in a popular magazine. A personal interview which Nadia had given revealing that one of her admirers had asked for a nude photograph of her which she had refused to give him. In the end she had posed for the photograph wearing only the diamond drop earrings and necklace that he had bought her. Nadia had been both amused and proud of the incident as Vanessa knew for she had boasted of it to her, telling her that the jewellery she had exchanged for the photograph was worth tens of thousands of pounds.

'I must admit I should enjoy seeing your delectable body arrayed in nothing more than fine jewels,' Jay continued softly, 'although in my case I think I should opt for sapphires, to match those magnificent eyes. Gavin has told you that I want you to pose with the team?'

The abrupt change of front startled her for a moment, her eyes widening slightly as she stared at him. 'Yes,' she agreed, 'he has mentioned it.'

'It will be the usual sort of thing,' Jay told her casually. 'You and the team in the Club's bath, you know the sort of thing.'

'You mean . . .' A horrible suspicion had just occurred to her.

'That this time I'm the one asking you to strip?' he mocked. 'That's right, although it isn't the first time you've been asked—or agreed.' Vanessa's mind reeled. It was true that Nadia had posed for several semi-nude shots, but she had never anticipated when Gavin talked of her appearing with the team that this was what Jay had in mind. Did Gavin know? Somehow she doubted it. She knew her brother would realise that there was no way she would ever agree to expose her body publicly in such a way.

'Something wrong?'

'Not a thing,' she told him carefully, 'but I'm afraid I can't agree to pose nude—or even semi-nude, if that's what you had in mind.'

'Why not? Afraid of over-exposure?' he taunted, laughing at her with those gold-rimmed eyes, reminding her more than ever of a ruthless predator in this eerie woodland setting with the light rapidly fading and the setting sun casting rays of gold through the trees.

'What's the matter?' he demanded softly. 'Isn't the publicity you'll be getting enough? Do you want the going rate as well?'

'I don't want to talk about it. I've said I won't do it and I won't.'

'I'm afraid you'll have to,' he told her quietly. 'It's written into the contract, or didn't you know?'

'I knew you wanted me to pose with the team, but not . . . not like that.'

'No?' His eyebrows rose, his face taking on an almost satanical expression in the half light. 'Come on, you can't expect me to believe that. It's standard procedure.'

'For you it might be, but not for me,' she told him with cold dignity, remembering too late the many occasions on which her cousin had displayed her body in just such provocative poses. At the time she had been half shocked, wondering how on earth Nadia could do it without feeling the embarrassment she knew would have crucified her.

'The photo session's booked for tomorrow,' he told her crisply. 'As a matter of fact I was on my way down to the lodge to tell you when I realised there was someone in the woods. We've had a few break-ins up at the house—tramps more than likely, so when I heard you crashing about . . .'

'I wasn't crashing!' she responded indigantly. How on earth was she going to convince him that nothing, but nothing would persuade her to pose as he wanted her to?

He seemed to think nothing of it, he even seemed impatient with her reluctance, a fact which was confirmed when he added sardonically, 'If it bothers you that much I can always make it up to you later—privately. As I've already said you have an extremely desirable body. You're cold,' he said abruptly, noticing that she had started to shiver. 'I'll walk you back to the lodge.'

She wanted to protest that she didn't want his company, but she sensed that he would ignore her. However, when the lodge came in sight, she pulled away from him. 'I can manage on my own now,' she told him stiffly, mortified when he laughed.

'Ah, I get the message. Well, sulk as much as you like my lovely, it won't make any difference,

I'm a businessman first, second and third my dear, and that contract stands.'

How on earth had she managed to get herself into this mess, Vanessa wondered wearily an hour later as she prepared for bed. Gavin had gone out and left a note saying not to expect him until much later, so that much as she longed to discuss the latest development with him it would have to wait until morning. Just when she thought the situation could get no worse, by some Machiavellian twist of fate it did. After lunch she had thought nothing could be worse than having to deceive Jay; now she knew how wrong she had been. She started to shiver. No matter how it was achieved she was not going to pose naked or even semi-naked with the team, contract or no contract. As she stepped out of the bath she realised she had left her cotton nightdress in the bedroom, quickly drying herself she wrapped the towel around herself and hurried into her room.

As she let the towel drop she caught sight of herself in the pier glass. Briefly she studied her body. Her breasts were high and firm, far more rounded than Nadia's, her waist narrow, and her stomach flat, her hips curved slightly, her legs long and slim. She closed her eyes and immediately became tormented with a vision of herself as she was now, but with huge sapphires decorating her ears, and another, suspended from a long fine chain, nestling between her breasts, glittering blue fire with every hesitant breath she took. Jay Courtland was a pagan to put such ideas into her head, to assault her defences with words and looks that conveyed subtly, but unmistakably, his desire for her. If it wasn't for the fact that he believed she was someone else, how easily she could give in to the promise she read in the dark gold of his eyes and the sweep of his hands across her body.

'You look pale Van, what's wrong?' Vanessa faced her brother across the breakfast table.

'Jay wants to do the publicity shots of me with the team today,' she told him tonelessly.

His hand reached out across the table, his fingers giving hers a reassuring squeeze. 'There's nothing to worry about. You'll be fine.'

'No, I won't, Gavin, because I won't be there. Jay wants you to photograph me nude,' she said flatly, watching the disbelief come and go in her brother's eyes before he burst out.

'He what? Van you must be wrong. He never said anything about that to me.'

'Well he did to me, and he probably never mentioned it to you because he assumed that you would know that's what he wanted. He was quite casual about it. Apparently it's the "done thing". He even reminded me about the contract when I told him I wouldn't do it.'

She saw the worry etch itself against Gavin's eyes as she imparted this last item of information and said quietly, 'Don't try persuading me to change my mind, Gavin, because I won't.'

'No, but what you could do is wear a swimsuit, one of those strapless ones, so that if you go deep enough in the pool it will look as though you might be nude. I'll do the shot so that we only see you from the top of your breasts upwards.'

Even the thought that people might assume that

she was naked without seeing made her shudder, but Gavin wouldn't let her object, and because she knew how much was at risk she eventually allowed herself to be persuaded.

'I doubt Jay will even be at the photographic session if that's what's worrying you,' Gavin reassured her. 'He'll be far too tied up with Supersport, so stop worrying and try to relax. Tension shows straight off in a photograph. There's nothing to worry about, I've given you my word . . .'

'You also gave it to me when you told me you'd tell Jay who I was,' Vanessa reminded him bitterly, wishing the harsh words unsaid when she caught his unhappy expression.

The drive to the football ground was a rather silent one, although Vanessa was conscious of Gavin glancing at her from time to time. When he drove into the town instead of taking the road which led direct to the ground Vanessa was slightly startled, until he pulled up and stopped in the narrow shopping street.

'You stay there,' he told her, 'I shan't be long.'

She watched him disappear into a shop specialising in continental beachwear and when he came back he tossed the package he was holding on to her lap. 'That should do the trick,' he told her. 'Want to go home first and try it on? There might not be facilities for you to change at the club. It is pretty primitive—something else that Jay intends to alter. As well as donating the new sports complex to the town he's having the club facilities modernised.'

'Hooray for him,' Vanessa said acidly as she

yanked on her seat belt. 'We had better go home then I can put this on. Have we got time?'

Gavin glanced at his watch and nodded his head. 'It won't take you long to change will it?'

It didn't. The swimsuit Gavin had bought was made of fine lycra and fitted her like a second skin, moulding around the slender curves of her body, the richly patterned fabric giving her an exotic appearance that was unfamiliar. The suit had detachable straps and was cleverly cut to reveal more of her body than it actually concealed, but at least it was some form of covering, even if she could never imagine herself wearing anything quite so daring on the beach.

'Okay?' Gavin asked her when she rejoined him in the car. 'Does that make you feel happier?' He laughed when he saw her expression. 'Poor Van, even if you had ambitions in that direction you'd never make a model, you're far too retiring; far too self-conscious.'

'Because I don't want to be photographed as though I were posing for some girlie mag?' Her tone was faintly acid. 'Not all models throw off their clothes at the command of a photographer. You might remember that none of this was my idea . . .'

'No, but you didn't correct Jay when you had the chance did you, that first time you met. You let him think you were Nadia.'

She couldn't argue with that and she bit her lip angrily, subsiding in her seat wishing the morning—and with it the photographic session—was over.

As Gavin had prophesied when they reached

the football ground there was no sign of Jay. Expelling a brief sigh of relief Vanessa smiled a greeting at the team manager, noticing that Gavin was careful not to introduce her.

'Bill Stoakes, Miss March,' he introduced himself, shaking Vanessa's hand heartily, 'Jay told us to expect you. The boys are all ready—more than ready,' he told her with a grin. 'They were supposed to be training this morning, but I couldn't get them to concentrate. They'll feel even less like doing so once they see you,' he added, admiring her with his eyes.

'Jay said he wanted the shots done in the boys' communal pool.' He pulled a wry face. 'Hardly a glamorous setting, but at least the water will be warm.'

'Not too warm, I hope,' Gavin interrupted, 'I don't want the lens fogging up with steam.'

Vanessa listened idly while the two men discussed photography which, apparently, was the team manager's hobby. Vanessa had never been particularly interested in the sport, although she recognised his face from photographs in the local paper. The team was all lined up to meet her when she walked into the changing rooms, the whistles and cheers bringing a faint tinge of colour to her face, although somehow, in its very obviousness and noisiness their appreciation of her was far less disturbing than one of Jay Courtland's mocking smiles. Most of the players were her own age or younger 'boys' as Bill Stoakes had called them, apart from one slightly older fair haired man whom she placed in his early thirties, and she felt her confidence returning as she listened to their teasing banter.

'Right,' Bill Stoakes called out, 'everyone in the pool. Tallest at the back! Johnny,' he called to one of the youngest players, a new recruit who had barely left school and who blushed profusely when he heard his name. 'I want you at the front, where I can see you.'

'Lucky Johnny,' one of his team mates called out.

Gavin was busily setting up his equipment and Bill Stoakes touched Vanessa lightly on the arm. 'I'm afraid we've no changing room proper for you, but if you'd like to use the shower to change in I've warned the lads that it's to be "no trespassing".'

Without looking at her brother, Vanessa stepped into the shower and quickly stripped down to her swimsuit, removing the straps, and not knowing whether to be glad or concerned that there was no mirror for her to inspect her appearance in. Taking a deep breath she stepped out in the changing room, telling herself that it would soon be over and that for the next hour she must forget that she was Vanessa and remember only that she was a model with a job to do.

It wasn't as bad as she had anticipated. The boys all gave an appreciative cheer when they saw her, but it was quickly quelled when Bill Stoakes frowned at them, and certainly nothing could have been more polite and respectful than their manner towards her when she joined them in the pool. As Gavin had instructed she let the water cover her swimsuit completely, only the upper curves of her breasts and her arms and shoulders visible to the camera. On impulse she had fastened her hair up on top of her head in a silky knot, much as she might have done if she were taking a shower, and Gavin left his camera to bend down and ease a few loose strands against her neck.

'Umm. It looks pretty good,' he murmured when he went back to the camera. 'Right everyone, look as though you're enjoying yourselves, Johnny put your arm round V ... Nadia's shoulders, Nadia, lean towards him and then back.' As she leaned back she started to overbalance slightly and the man standing behind her steadied her, his hand on her shoulder, her momentary panic turning to a grateful smile. 'That's fantastic,' Gavin called out. 'Great. Smile at him again ...' She was so busy concentrating on the instructions Gavin was giving her that there wasn't time for her to feel nervous. 'That was great,' Gavin told her enthusiastically as he helped her up out of the pool. 'You can rest for a moment and then we'll try a few more. This time I want a shot of you lying on top of the water with the boys holding you.'

'What about the swimsuit?' Vanessa asked him nervously.

'What?' Gavin frowned, plainly so wrapped up in his work that her meaning hadn't penetrated. 'Oh that,' he dismissed lightly. 'I don't think Jay's going to quibble when he sees the shots I've got. Personally I think you look more sexy wearing the suit than you would do without it ...'

'But I seem to remember saying expressly that you weren't to do so.'

Both of them swung round at the sound of Jay's voice, Gavin frowning, Vanessa tense and pale as she glanced upwards along the lean lines of his body, unable to prevent herself from doing so, even though common sense told her to keep her eyes averted. Today he was dressed formally in a dark business suit, and a crisp white shirt. A tie, discreetly patterned to tone with his suit provided a contrast to the stark whiteness of his shirt. A strange feeling of weakness seemed to invade her body. It began as nerve prickling tension low in her stomach and ran like wildfire through her veins, turning her muscles to cotton wool, leaving her rooted to the spot conscious of his slow, careless inspection of her body, and the silence that had fallen on the room, but trapped within the magnetism of his gaze and completely unable to move. Today his eyes weren't gold, but a hard dark yellow; predator's eyes, and she shrank beneath the glittering determination she could read in his hooded gaze.

Gavin had retreated to fiddle with his camera. Coward, Vanessa thought bitterly, knowing there was no point in turning to her brother for aid.

'Well?' he queried, standing easily, hands on his hips as he waited for her response. For all the world as though she were a naughty schoolgirl, she thought irately. The sudden jolt of anger freed her to respond. Her chin lifted, her eyes flashing warning sparks at him as she turned to face him, casually picked up a towel from the chair, wrapping it round her body with a cool confidence she was far from feeling.

'And I thought I told you that I wouldn't do nude or even semi-nude poses. If that was what you wanted you picked the wrong person.'

'On the contrary,' Jay interposed smoothly, 'I

have picked the right person. Why so coy?' he demanded tauntingly. 'Surely you haven't forgotten posing for that centrespread—when was it? Only six months or so ago, if my memory serves me right. I certainly haven't forgotten it, although I must admit,' his eyes slid insolently over her body, bringing a quick rush of colour to her pale skin, before resting meaningfully on her breasts, 'your figure is decidedly more voluptuous than I realised.'

How could her cousin expose herself to these sorts of insults; this casual acceptance of her body as a commodity? It made Vanessa shudder with revulsion. 'Now get back in the tub,' he told her in a soft voice, 'and Gavin will finish the session.' She took a step back, gasping as his fingers suddenly locked on her arms. 'But we'll finish it the way I want it, Nadia, like this.' Her towel was twitched away and with one deft movement Jay grasped the top of her swimsuit just beneath her arms, pulling it down to her waist, leaving her breasts fully exposed to his gaze. Her back was to the pool and the assembled team, but the very quality of their silence told her they must be aware that something was going on.

'Now,' Jay said softly, his breath just grazing her temple as he bent her head, his grip on her arms the only thing that stopped her from crossing her arms protectively over her breasts. She felt mortified with embarrassment, humiliated beyond belief, panic flaring to life in the pit of her stomach, all her defences urging escape. She could feel Jay's fingers tense into her skin, fear tearing at her composure. She wouldn't do what he wanted; she

couldn't; she would die first ... she would ...
'Now,' he repeated, 'do you join them willingly, or
do I have to throw you in? That would make a
good picture, although I doubt that many of your
admirers would believe your reluctance. What was
it you said to that reporter from the *Daily Globe*?
"Variety is the spice of life"? and "It's impossible
to have too much of a good thing, and as far as
I'm concerned, sex is the very best!"'

'No.' Vanessa moaned the denial through stiff
lips, panic leaping from nerve ending to nerve
ending. She felt Jay bend towards her, and knew
he meant what he said. Her toes curled in mute
protest as his hands slid to her waist. He mustn't
do it ... he ... When the room started to sway
round her at first she thought he had picked her
up and expected with every second to feel him
striding towards the pool, but the room was going
strangely dark, and there was a dull sound in her
ears, as though water were rushing down a
waterfall, a distant muted sound, overlaid by the
sharp query in Gavin's voice, the impression of
swift movements, of darkness closing round her
like a welcome cloak hiding her shame and
anguish from her and from everyone else.

CHAPTER FOUR

'It's all right Nadia, you just fainted, that's all.'
Why was Gavin calling her 'Nadia', and why that
touch of warning in his voice. Vanessa struggled to
sit up, and found she was lying on a hard bench
wrapped in a huge towel that hampered her
movements. She glanced round, and recognised
the changing room, now empty apart from Gavin,
and Jay Courtland. Jay! Her heart gave an
agonising leap and seemed to lodge somewhere in
her throat. Tears pricked her eyes.

'Go and see if you can find her a glass of water
or even better a cup of tea,' she heard Jay ordering
Gavin in a cool voice. She wanted to protest, to
demand that Gavin stay with her, and as though
he guessed her thoughts, Jay turned from his
scrutiny of Gavin's retreating back to say curtly,
'You're perfectly safe, I'm not about to rape you if
that's what you're thinking.'

He followed her glance down her towel-
enshrouded body and laughed sardonically, 'It's
all right, you're perfectly respectable, swimsuit back
in place.'

Her eyes met his, hectic colour staining her too
pale face. 'Who . . .'

'I put it back, if that's what you want to know.'
He saw her colour fluctuate and just for a second
his own skin darkened, a faint tide of red,
sweeping up under the darkness of his tan, his eyes

glowing that burning gold which made her body tremble so badly. 'It's okay, I've got the message—at last.' He told her curtly. He turned away from her slightly, his neck stiff with a tension she found it hard to analyse. Was he angry because she had defeated him by fainting. Or had she defeated him?

She glanced wildly at the pool, and said huskily 'You're not . . .'

'What? Going through that performance all over again? No, I'm not. It seems I owe you an apology.' He said it tersely, hands thrust into his pockets as he moved away from her and leaned against the wall. 'You obviously meant what you said. You'll have to forgive me for not taking you seriously before, but going on past evidence . . . What happened? Did you suddenly wake up one morning and decide you'd made enough money from selling your skin to be able to stop doing it, or . . .' He saw her face before she could conceal her expression from him, and cursed softly, coming to her side, where he dropped down on one knee and took hold of her hand. 'You're cold. Where's that damned cousin of yours? Forget what I just said Nadia,' he told her. 'The first time I saw you you threw me off course. You're woman of the world enough to know exactly what I mean.' He grimaced. 'I haven't exactly lived as a monk, but in the past I've always been able to take what I wanted, and then leave, with you . . .' His eyes darkened and he bent towards her saying huskily, 'Let's just say I want you as I've wanted no other woman, but you have my word that I won't try and coerce you. My pride wouldn't let me. I suppose there've been so many women in my life who say what they don't mean, I can't recognise the truth when I hear it any longer. How do you feel about us starting again, preferably from that moment when you told me to strip off. Let me take you out to dinner tonight?'

She was just about to refuse when Gavin returned. 'I think your cousin should go home now,' Jay told him. 'I'm taking her out to dinner tonight.' Gavin glanced from Jay's unreadable face to Vanessa's pale, anxious one, but said nothing, waiting until Jay had left before voicing his concern.

'Is that a good idea Van?' he asked her worriedly. 'Why does he want to take you out?'

'For all the usual reasons,' she told him dryly, adding with a brief, painful smile, 'I believe he wants to go to bed with me.'

'You mean he wants to have an affair with you?' Gavin said bluntly. 'Don't get any romantic ideas Van, he's a man who's made his views on marriage pretty well known, and they're all of the "why confine yourself exclusively to one, when there are so many ready, willing and able", brand. Remember, he thinks you're Nadia, someone as experienced and determinedly footloose as he is himself. You aren't equipped to deal with a man like that. He'll hurt you—and very badly. Don't get involved with him Van. I know I said he was ready for marriage—but I meant a marriage of the business variety—not a love-match. I doubt that's an emotion he recognises!'

It was nothing she hadn't already told herself and yet some deep feminine part of her cried out for her to give in to her inner yearnings. She was twenty-two and had never had a lover, might never again meet a man who made her feel the way Jay did. All right so all he wanted was an affair. If she kept that in mind couldn't she minimise the ultimate pain? Wouldn't it be worth the suffering ahead to experience the ecstasy of being held in his arms?

'You're forgetting something aren't you?' she asked her brother dryly. He looked confused and she elucidated. 'I'm not Vanessa any longer, I'm Nadia—remember?'

'Outwardly, you may be, but inside you're still Van,' he warned her, 'and I shouldn't like to be in your shoes if he should find out. Can't you see Van?' Gavin said earnestly. 'He wants you because he thinks you are Nadia. You read the gossip columns, you know as well as I do, the sort of women he goes for, sophisticated, worldly women as adept at playing the game as he is himself. Commitment, emotions they don't even begin to figure in their calculations. He doesn't want you,' Gavin told her brutally. 'If he knew the real you, who you really are he'd run a mile. He wants Nadia.'

She wanted to deny his allegations but the words stuck in her throat. Jay had never met Nadia; it was *her* he wanted. But did he? Would he if he knew the truth? Was he attracted to the glamour of Nadia's image? It was *her* body he wanted to possess she reminded herself, not her mind or her heart, and yet still that same inner yearning remained; that compulsion to go to him and be whatever he wanted her to be. It wasn't love; it couldn't be, because love came with knowing and understanding; no it was merely a physical hunger; a potent virus she had contracted which would run its course and then go. The fact of her virginity she pushed to the back of her mind. These days when girls were so much more active; when life had changed in so many directions surely it was not still possible for a man to know whether a woman was a virgin or not. She knew she should have experienced shame at the direction her thoughts were taking, but all she did feel was a fiercely elemental hunger; a need that coursed through her body, taking precedence over everything else. She wanted Jay just as much as he seemed to want her, with an intensity she ought to have experienced during adolescence but had not. So, she shrugged mentally, she was just a late developer. Jay was not going to be a permanent feature in her life, but they would be lovers. Just as long as she did not allow herself to become emotionally involved with him she would be quite safe.

On an impulse it was hard for her to analyse she dressed for her dinner date with Jay in one of the new outfits Gavin had bought for her, a simple shirt style silk dress which buttoned down the front, its deep blue colour matching her eyes, the side slits in the straight skirt giving provocative glimpses of the length of her legs as she moved. A narrow gold belt cinched her small waist, the buttons unfastened to just above her breasts, the full sleeves caught up into tight cuffs at the wrists, emphasising the slender femininity of her body. A gold chain which had been a present from her parents caught the light as she moved, her hair a perfumed cloud of black silk, curving just below her shoulders. Gold sandals and a small clutch bag completed her outfit, and before she left her room she checked her make-up in her mirror worriedly. She was wearing more than she would normally have done and had spent some time shadowing and shading her eyes, and had been rather surprised by the result; their glowing sapphire colour was reflected in her dress, the delicate kohl outline she had given them and the mascara she had used making them seem twice as large as usual, and certainly far more provocative. A delicate blackcurrant lip gloss tinted her mouth to a warm sheen, and Gavin raised his eyebrows a little when she went downstairs. 'Definitely well past the chrysalis stage,' he commented as she looked anxiously at him. 'I only hope you know what you're doing? This isn't some callow boy you're going out with Van. He means business by the look of him and he won't take kindly to playing the sort of stop go games you're used to indulging in. He's way, way out of your class,' he told her frankly, 'Like you're in the infants, and he's reached senior grade. In fact he's beyond it. I'd feel much happier if you didn't go.'

'Isn't it rather late to start playing the protective brother?' Vanessa asked him dryly, feeling guilty when she saw him flush. 'Gavin, it *is* time I grew up a little you know,' she told him.

'Perhaps, but I'd feel one hell of a lot happier if you weren't using Nadia's reputation as a means of doing it. There's growing up and growing up——' he broke off as they both heard the sound of a car. 'Here's your escort by the sound of it.'

The car stopped, and Vanessa felt her breath locking in her throat as she heard a car door closing and then the sound of footsteps on the path. Jay was dressed casually in black jeans and a matching black silk shirt, the top buttons carelessly undone. His eyes seemed to glow as he looked at her, an indefinable tension filling the room.

'Ready?'

She nodded her head, preceding him through the door, breathing in the cool, fresh scent of the evening. A soft breeze played over her skin, the air full of the scent of roses; dusk was just starting to fall.

'I thought we'd eat at the Harlequin,' Jay told her when he had helped her into the car and settled himself at her side. 'I've heard it's quite good.'

The Harlequin was a newly opened wine bar-cum-restaurant which had an excellent reputation, and which was somewhere Vanessa had never been before. It was several miles' drive away, a converted water mill, with its wheel and the mill pool still in existence. The pool had been stocked with beautiful Japanese koi carp and the gardens dotted with tables and chairs for outdoor eating during the day. The restaurant had been the venue for several weddings since its opening and as they swept into the gravelled forecourt, Vanessa glimpsed coloured lanterns illuminating the gardens. A trellised archway led through to them and to the restaurant, the scent of roses filling her nostrils once again as they walked under it. Their perfume was similar to that which she used on her skin and a frisson of awareness shivered through her when Jay took her elbow and guided her towards the restaurant.

She asked him to order for her, too caught up in the powerful tug of her emotions to want to eat. Just sitting opposite him looking at him made her body weak with longing. It was a physical effort not to reach out and touch him; not to trace the exposed flesh of his throat with her tongue, not to . . .

'Would you like an aperitif while we're waiting?' She shook her head, watching the warm, knowing smile that curved his mouth. 'I think you're right,' he said softly. 'Tonight my appetite needs no priming either. Tell me about yourself. All I know is what I've read.'

'There's nothing to tell,' she responded honestly, 'besides I'd rather talk about you.'

'Would you? Or has someone already told you how flattering the male animal finds it to talk about himself. What would you like to know? How a raw fourth division football player made it to the top of the financial ladder? Not by taking any short cuts,' he told her flatly, 'but certainly with a lot of pain.' He glanced round the restaurant, surveying its subdued lighting, the other diners, expensively and elegantly dressed, the muted sound of their voices reaching them above the strains of the piped music. 'Fifteen years ago I'd never set foot in a place like this, nor imagined I might. Those boys you saw today are worldly sophisticates compared with me at their age. I'd been nowhere, done nothing, an inmate of an institution who didn't even know which cutlery to use, who was terrified of putting a step wrong, but like everyone else I learned. Sometimes the hard way.'

'You've never been married?'

His eyebrows rose as though he was surprised by the gaucheness of her comment, certainly not one that Nadia would ever have made. 'I came pretty close to it once, until I heard my bride-to-be describing me as "pretty grotty raw material which she would have to work hard on to make passable." ' He saw the shocked sympathy in her eyes and laughed harshly, "Oh don't feel sorry for me—I don't, it was a lucky escape. She was the daughter of a viscount and I was foolish enough to believe we were in love. What she was in love with was herself and the glamour attached to being engaged to a personality. I met her just after I was picked for the English squad at a press party, but as I say I soon learned, and she was right, there were an awful lot of rough edges in those days. You wouldn't even have glanced at me. I had no money, no sophistication, nothing . . .'

'Oh but . . .' she broke off as their first course arrived, not wanting to make herself look even more gauche by admitting that as far as she was concerned he must always have possessed that driving maleness that drew her like a moth to certain doom. No doubt she was not the first woman to sense and be dazzled by it, nor would she be the last.

'Everyone feels insecure and vulnerable at that age,' she said instead when the waiter had served them. 'I think the agonies of the teens are common to every generation.'

'Not to you, surely,' he drawled, 'Gavin was telling me that you were a beauty at fourteen with more boys flocking round you than wasps round a honey pot. You were the local beauty queen for four years running . . .'

'That doesn't mean I don't know what it feels like to be an outsider,' she flashed back defensively, 'to know what it's like to be rejected to . . .'

'Yes, of course, I suppose in your case your beauty and your sexuality would set you apart. You must have inspired seething jealousy in more than one female heart, but we both came through it and made it, although I'm surprised that in your case it didn't leave a much tougher shell than it has done. You're still amazingly vulnerable, astoundingly so really. It's almost as though you're two different people; the image you project as a model is so very different from the one you're projecting right now. Everything's the same, but somehow different. When I look at you there's none of that open sexuality that's such a feature of your pictures.'

Vanessa's heart started to thump. He was far too astute, coming far too close to stumbling on the truth . . . She forced a smile, tossing her head, narrowing her eyes and pouting slightly. 'Like this, do you mean?' she asked huskily, her pulses suddenly leaping as his eyes darkened to deep topaz.

'Something like that,' he agreed thickly. 'Only it looks far more potent in the flesh than it ever does on film. A look like that could make a man do some very dangerous things.'

Suddenly she felt reckless enough to say softly, 'Tell me about them,' the breath jerking painfully into her throat as Jay reached across the table and grasped her hand. 'Let's forget about eating, food isn't what I'm hungry for anyway. Come back with me to my place Nadia . . .'

There was no reason why she should be so tongue-tied, it was what she had been expecting all evening, nevertheless she gulped at her wine, drinking it quickly, hoping he hadn't seen the quick betraying blush stealing over her skin. 'Don't let's play games with one another,' Jay was muttering huskily. 'You know how much I want you; how much I have wanted you right from the first. Just as you want me.' His eyes held hers and wouldn't let her escape. She drained her glass of wine suddenly giddy from a mixture of excitement and tension, her whispered, 'Yes,' thick and unfamiliar on her tongue.

In no time at all they were back outside, the welcome breeze wafting over her over-heated skin. To her surprise, instead of heading straight for the car, Jay drew along one of the sheltered paths, stopping in the shelter of the wisteria that cloaked one side of the building, his strong hands cupping her face, his fingers sliding into her hair as he tilted her head back. 'You don't know how much I've wanted this,' he muttered thickly against her throat, burying his mouth in her skin, his lips hot and dry as they burned like a brand across the paleness of her throat, moving upwards as his urgency found an echo in her, her fingers locking behind his head as she arched against him, inviting the plunder of her exposed throat. Small sounds of pleasure rose from deep inside her, muffled against the dark thickness of his hair, as her body caught fire from his and she was lost in compulsive response to him, drowning in the heavy, dark seas of passion, pressing her lips feverishly against his skin, feeling the perspiration break out on it, as his hands slid down her body, grasping her hips, letting her feel the reality of his arousal, his teeth tugging gently on her bottom lip, and then less gently, as she yielded completely, matching the fierce passion she could feel racing through him, shocked by the sudden inrush of cool night air, when he abruptly released her.

'You're making me behave like a love-crazed adolescent,' he told her, rubbing his thumb along her swollen mouth as though he couldn't bring himself to break all physical contact with her. Her lower body ached for the incitement so recently proferred by his, but as she made a small convulsive movement towards him, he stepped back, his smile wry. 'We'd better not. Another few seconds of that, and I'd have taken you right here, like an inexperienced boy.'

'And?' She could hardly believe she had actually murmured the small teasing invitation.

'And,' he said in a deep voice, 'when I do take you I don't want it to be a hurried, brief act of physical release, like a starving man reaching indiscriminately for his food. No, when we make love, it will be as gourmets ... I want to taste every silken inch of your body, to sample each one of the delights I know you can give me.' As he spoke he drew her out of the shadows, towards the car, stopping briefly in the lee of the wall, to add roughly, 'but before we go...' His fingers unfastened two more of the buttons on her dress, the moonlight gleaming whitely on the silken valley he had just exposed, the touch of his fingers, stroking aside the silk that covered her breasts, tormentingly arousing, her small gasp of pleasure heating the silence that enfolded them both as he bent his head and followed the path of his fingers with his mouth exploring her tender shape, gently at first and then more urgently as he encountered the barrier of her delicate lace bra, pushing it aside impatiently so that he could savour the hard bud of flesh first with his tongue and then with the hot demand of his mouth, his slow groan of pleasure silenced against her skin.

'Come with me, Nadia,' he groaned huskily when he released her. 'Stay with me tonight...'

Nadia! At the sound of her cousin's name on the lips of the man she now knew she loved, Vanessa trembled. Now was the moment to draw back; the only chance she would get to take the safe path to sanity, but it was the higher path that called to her, the dangerous route to the peaks which lured her on, promising untold pleasures ... and she took it. Firmly closing her mind to sanity and common sense, her eyes shining with the love she hoped Jay would not recognise, she said softly, 'Yes please.'

The drive to his apartment in a new building on the outskirts of the town was a tense one. They made desultory conversation; Jay telling her that the apartment was his, but that he only intended living there until the manor was finished. When they pulled up outside a stark concrete block

Vanessa's heart plunged. She had been so caught up in her physical feelings that she had forgotten, or pushed to the back of her mind, the differences between them. She revered age and tradition; Jay was a modernist to his finger tips, a man who would rip down a lovely building like the manor without a qualm, a man who would tear apart her heart and destroy her life if he ever found out that she had deceived him. Panic flared to life inside her as he helped her out of the car, and as though he sensed the indecision curling through her, his fingers grasped her wrist as he led her into the foyer and pressed the button to summon the lift.

It deposited them in a small square hallway, painted stark white, its coldness relieved only by the wall of green plants, their leaves reflected in the mirror behind them.

She waited tensely as Jay unlocked the door, and reached for the light. They were in a small hallway painted a soft beige, a rich Persian rug glowing jewel bright on the floor. It was so unexpected that she stared blindly at it before she realised that Jay was holding open another door, waiting for her to precede him inside.

'I know it's a bit bleak,' he said gesturing to the room, 'but it is only temporary.' One wall was taken up entirely with bookshelves stacked with books, the floor carpeted in a warm rust shade to tone in with the soft cream walls. A leather chesterfield upholstered in rich bronze was drawn up in front of the fireplace, a coffee table strategically placed close by it. At the back of the room were more shelves, holding a stereo system and a selection of records.

'I'll go and get us both a drink,' Jay told her. 'It's in the study, I won't be a moment, make yourself at home.' There were some prints on the wall, by an artist Vanessa didn't recognise, but so skilfully drawn that she guessed they must be valuable, and she wandered from them towards the bookshelves, amazed by the catholic taste they revealed. There was everything from Shakespeare to Chekov, from Dickens to Dick Francis; textbooks jostling with novels; a series of children's books she herself could vividly remember reading, books on football, on chess . . .

A step behind her alerted her to Jay's return. He was carrying two glasses brimming with pale amber liquid.

'What did you do?' she joked, feeling self-conscious, 'buy a job lot from a library that was closing down?'

His face closed immediately, his eyes cold and remote. 'No, as a matter of fact they're all books that I've read. Hasn't anyone ever told you that it's the one way the poor and oppressed can escape from the narrow poverty of their lives. We were lucky at the orphanage, we had plenty of books given to us. I soon discovered how easy it was to lose myself in a good story, then when I grew older I discovered how much one could learn from the same source.'

She hadn't thought of him as a reader; nor had she imagined he would have the taste or the feel for good things to furnish a room as this one was furnished, and as though he had read her mind he said sardonically, 'Even rough diamonds collect some polish on their way through life you know.'

'You chose these things yourself?' Her glance encompassed the whole room, and he smiled grimly. 'Why not? I'm the one who has to live with them. I don't go for designer room settings, all clinical and correct. I like the things around me that I'm familiar with. I bought those prints with the first cheque I received as a football player. I bought my first stocks and shares just after we won the Cup. A man uses the talents he's given to succeed in life, but being a sportsman doesn't necessarily go hand in hand with atrophy of the brain; being a businessman does not preclude an interest in the arts.'

She had been guilty of misjudging him and he was letting her know it, and there was no way in which she could apologise. 'Like some music?' He walked towards the stereo system, but suddenly the magic had gone out of the evening.

'No I think I ought to be going after all,' she said awkwardly, 'I . . .'

'You're having second thoughts?' he handed her her glass. 'Well I'm not going to force you to stay. What's the matter? Did I only appeal when you thought you were slumming, is that it? A bit of rough? Is that what appeals to you?'

'No!' Her voice was horrified, and she took a long swallow of her drink, hoping to steady herself. The spirit burned the back of her throat making her choke. She took another gulp, forcing herself to meet his eyes. They were glowing topaz as they always did when he was angry. Cat's eyes, predator's eyes, and she had just deprived him of his prey. 'I must go Jay,' she said huskily, draining her glass and putting it down, her eyes darting to the closed door. 'Thank you for taking me out but . . .'

'In a minute,' he said softly, 'You can give me your bread and butter thank yous when I've given you something to thank me for.'

She was in his arms before she could move, but there was none of the violence in his embrace that she had anticipated and tensed herself against. Instead his tongue stroked slowly over her lips, softening their tense outline, his hands moving seductively over her body, his caresses slowly becoming more sensual. Now it was his mouth that touched her dry lips, moving seductively across their tremulous outline, his tongue easing them apart, exploring the soft sensitivity of her lower lip and then moving moistly down to the tense contours of her throat, undermining her willpower, his hand pushing aside the soft silk to capture her breast at the same moment as his mouth closed over the betraying pulse beating desperately beneath her skin. 'I don't think you really want to leave,' he told her, his mouth destroying her defences, returning to tease and torment her trembling lips, urging them apart, urging them to welcome his determined invasion, urging them to utter broken words of first denial and then admission, that he spoke the truth, and that there was nowhere she would rather be than here in his arms. 'Say it Nadia,' he muttered against her mouth. 'Tell me you're going to stay.'

She closed her eyes and told him, returning his kisses with tiny, fierce ones of her own, shivering as she felt his immediate response, burying her mouth in the salt warmth of his throat as he swung her off the floor, and carried her through into the darkness of his bedroom.

CHAPTER FIVE

SLOWLY, almost as though he took pleasure in deliberately drawing out his self-imposed task Jay undressed her, only allowing his fingers to touch her skin briefly. Did he share the exquisite sense of anticipation building inside her, Vanessa wondered; did he too experience that same coiling, thrusting urgency that tensed her body with sensual hunger, wrapping her skin with tongues of fire whose heat could only be quenched by the caress of skin on skin, of mouths and then bodies melding two people into one.

She moaned low in her throat and heard Jay say huskily, 'Hush ... I know, I know ... but the pleasure will be all the sweeter if we sharpen it a little with the tang of denial now. Show me what you like,' he urged her, leaning on his side next to her, stroking the outline of her with one hand, the other propping up his head. 'Show me ...' he bit delicately into her shoulder feeling the shudders of pleasure she could not control, stroking the silky skin which still bore the imprint of his teeth with long fingers, his mouth trailing upwards along her throat, his tongue investigating the vulnerable hollow of her ear. 'Show me and tell me.' His lips were against her ear, frissons of electricity jolting to her nerve endings, her body arching impatiently towards him. 'So very responsive, so infinitely pleasurable to touch. It arouses me just to see the pleasure dawn in your eyes. Do you like this?' His mouth found her breast, his tongue caressing its aching peak, his breathing suddenly accelerating. She reached blindly towards him feeling his heart thudding erratically against her palm, not sure if the moan that escaped her lips was one of pleasure or despair, the twisting movements of her body against him as she tried to tell him that his touch was too intimate, too soon, seeming only to incite him to further intimacies, the warm moist possession of his mouth against her breast sending fierce pangs of pleasure darting through her body, the hands she had raised to push him away, curling into the thick darkness of his hair, moving down over his shoulders, holding him to her while she arched unashamedly beneath him, not pushing him away, but imprisoning him against her. Her breath was coming in deep harsh gasps, fine tremors shuddering through her body, her head thrown back against the pillows, her primary feeling when his erotic possession of her breasts ceased one of intense loss.

'There is no need to hold me quite so fiercely,' he drawled unsteadily as he lifted his head to stare up at her, 'I have no intentions of leaving. I wanted you from the first moment I saw you. I knew then we would be good together, but I had no idea you were going to be so enticingly responsive. His fingers brushed lightly against her nipple, her body moving feverishly against him in response, her eyes begging him unashamedly to caress her and go on caressing her. 'You still haven't told me what you like,' he reminded her in a slow husky drawl. 'Is it this?' His mouth found the tender curve of her elbow, the rasp of his tongue against the sensitised flesh almost unbearable. 'Or this?' His tongue trailed down her arm, his eyes so dark with arousal they might have been black. 'Surely you have a preference? Are you going to tell me what it is, or do I have to find out?' He shifted her slightly as he spoke, kneeling beside her, his fingers drawing erotic patterns against the slight swell of her stomach, the response of her flesh to his touch something that suddenly burned out of control, her body twisting and moving beneath his hand, the harsh aching sound of her own breathing something she could barely recognise.

'Jay please . . .'

'Please what?' He moved again, his hands cupping her breasts, his tongue slowly anointing the pink crests of each in turn, with fierce concentration, until his gaze suddenly shifted to her face and he muttered something deep in his throat before pulling her into his arms. 'Are you deliberately trying to drive me crazy?' he demanded hoarsely. 'Touch me.' He groaned the command into her throat, lifting her hands to his body. 'Touch me, kiss me, pleasure me the way I've imagined you doing from the first time we met.'

His shirt had come unfastened almost to the waist, and obeying him blindly, Vanessa let her fingertips trace the ridged muscle beneath the warm flesh, following the dark vee of hair which tapered down to his waist, and beyond, her moan of frustration mingling with his when she came to the barrier of his jeans. He rolled back to allow her easier access to the fastening, his lips exploring the curve of her shoulder, his hands still caressing her body. The intimacy of what she was doing suddenly caught up with her, making her feel awkward and uncertain, her fingers fumbling, until he cursed and pulled away, tearing savagely at his belt.

With only the moonlight to illuminate the room, sounds seemed preternaturally loud, the impatient rustle of clothing intensified a hundredfold, until it suddenly stopped. 'Aren't you going to help me?' She heard the impatience in his voice, and its faint thickening. Of course he would expect her to help; to participate; perhaps even to make the sort of advances to him she would, if she were actually Nadia.

'It's these damned jeans,' he complained as he sat up. 'I think they must have shrunk.'

She had noticed how closely they clung to his thighs in the car, and a shiver trembled through her as she moved automatically to the floor, kneeling there to grip the dark fabric at the ankle, and then as her embarrassment left her, and desire quickened inside her once again, holding her in its heady coil, reached up to ease the taut fabric away from his body. Her nails accidentally grazed the muscles of his thigh, his swiftly indrawn breath stilling her movements. As though realising her inability to help him any further, Jay completed the task himself, while she knelt at his side unable to drag her gaze away from the masculine perfection of his body, unable to prevent tremulous fingers from reaching out to touch the crisp, dark hair shadowing his thigh. He tensed convulsively, meeting her dark, bewildered eyes with hotly gold ones, no longer making any attempt to conceal from her the intensity of his desire for her.

A virginal fear she had never expected to experience trembled through her and she wanted to tell him that he would be her first lover. To stop the words from being uttered she pressed her hot face unthinkingly against the cool flesh of his thighs. Her action was an instinctive one, designed to hide her face and her thoughts from him, but the sensation of his skin beneath her cheek and the warm male scent of him which invaded her senses, obliterated her doubts as instantly as though they had been blasted by dynamite.

Above her she heard Jay mutter something unintelligible and then she felt his fingers tangling in the black silk of her hair, his mouth against the soft skin of her nape, his body tensing beneath her fingers as they explored his male shape. Her body seemed to have developed a will and experience over which her mind had no control, her lips scattering tremulous kisses against his thighs, her body revelling in his primitive response, her heart thudding in concert with the hurried, uneven beats of his. He muttered something into her skin, a plea, a protest, she couldn't tell which, only that his hands had slid from her hair down over her skin to her waist and that he was lifting her, forcing her away from the heated warmth of his body, his voice thick and slurred, the harshness of his breathing a delicious counterpart to her own accelerated pulses.

'I want you. Dear God how I want you,' he breathed against her mouth. His tongue traced the outline of her lips, teasing, arousing her until she was aching for the possession of his kiss, her eyes dark with the frustration he was deliberately building as he played with her soft lips—one moment gentle, the next passionately rough. She wanted to lose herself completely in him, Vanessa thought hazily, to be so completely part of him they would never be apart again.

'You're a very desirable and a very, very dangerous young woman, do you know that?' he murmured into her ear. 'Very dangerous.' She wrapped her arms round him in mute response, her fingertips trailing down over his spine, his sigh of pleasure shivering across her nerve endings. 'The day I met you really was my lucky day . . .'

'I can't be the first woman you've wanted.' She said it huskily, knowing she was saying the words more for her own protection than because she wanted to hear him admit it.

'No, not the first,' he agreed, bending to find the vulnerably responsive spot where her neck joined her shoulder, and teasing it with his teeth until she murmured his name and arched softly against him. 'But there are degrees of wanting, and on a scale of nought to ten, what I feel about you goes way, way over the top of the register.'

'And that's bad?' Why was she tormenting herself like this? She already knew that all there could be between them was a brief affair, why make herself unhappy before she needed to be.

'Not in this case.' Her spirits flew upwards, only to plummet back down to earth as he murmured, 'That's what I meant about getting lucky. You could have been some small town girl who didn't know the rules of the game, but you're not and you do.'

'You mean . . . you mean no commitments?' She already knew the answer, but for some reason she had to ask the question.

'Not of the forever kind; not the kind that demands a ring and promises that no man can possibly keep. If more people accepted that that's how life is there'd be less kids around being brought up in institutions, unwanted by their fathers, an embarrassment to their mothers. We know the right way to play the game, don't we? No commitment, no tears when it's over, just the enjoying of the pleasure we can give one another while it lasts, and we can give one another pleasure, can't we?'

His mouth moved down over her body when he finished speaking, tracing the soft curves of her breast. Another moment and she would be lost completely; already her body was moving compulsively to the urgent thrust of his hips. And yet, despite her love for him, her physical need for completion, she still wanted to cry; to beg him to tell her that he loved her. To lie to her, she thought wretchedly. Dear God what a fool she had been. She had known how it would be right from the start, but she had gone ahead blindly, mulishly, telling herself that . . . She felt the sudden tension in Jay's body, his head lifting in sudden concentration.

'Phone,' he told her briefly, moving away from her. Vanessa could hear it ringing herself now, and she shivered as she watched him walk into the living room to answer it. He was gone only seconds. She was still trying to come to terms with the abrupt cessation of their love-making, with the withdrawal of his body from hers, when he came back, casually reaching for his jeans and starting to pull them on. There was none of the desire in his eyes that she had seen earlier. Now they looked hard and angrily alert.

'There's been a break in up at the manor,' he told her curtly. 'Some local hotheads, they've started a fire. That was the police. Everything's under control apparently, but I still need to be there.'

'I'll come with you, you can drop me off at the lodge on the way,' Vanessa suggested, hurriedly pulling on her own clothes. The mood of the evening had been broken, and she knew she could not endure to lie here in Jay's bed, waiting for his return, hearing over and over again in her mind those cool words which had totally destroyed her frail hopes.

He frowned and then shrugged. 'I suppose you may as well. There's no telling how long this will take.'

She was surprised when she glanced at her watch to discover how relatively early it still was. Only just after twelve.

As they drove up to the lodge lights streamed from every window. In the distance Vanessa could hear sounds, although there was no evidence, as she had dreaded that the manor was being totally consumed by flames. Gavin came striding out of the lodge as she opened the car door, smiling a greeting at them both. There were smudges of smoke on his face, and as he approached them

Vanessa caught the acrid smell of burning on his clothes.

'How bad is it?' Jay asked grittily. 'All the police told me was that there'd been a break in and that the place was on fire.'

'Not too much damage so far,' Gavin reassured him. 'They've caught the culprits, two lads who were living rough. They'd broken in and started a fire. They were discovered when the police did their nightly check—fortunately before things got out of control, but it's an old house and the fire brigade want to make sure there's no chance of it starting up again. It looks like being a long night,' he added, turning to Vanessa. 'How about manning the kettle for us? It's hot, thirsty work.'

'If you're going back I'll give you a lift down there,' Jay offered to Gavin. Her presence was forgotten Vanessa recognised sadly, her importance diminished; and for the first time she saw very clearly the meagreness of the role any woman must accept in Jay's life. He was a man with a strong sexual drive, capable of giving the woman in his arms intense physical pleasure, but he was not prepared to make any emotional commitment. He had said himself, although he didn't know it, that if he had met her as she really was he would never have got intimately involved with her. But he *did* want her, Vanessa reminded herself stubbornly, as the two men drove off and she walked up to the house. His childhood had scarred him, but surely not beyond all healing. So what would cure him? The love of a good woman? She smiled rather cynically at her own folly. Good women obviously did not figure very high on Jay's list of priorities for his life.

The rest of the night passed in a blur. The fire, although under control, had been serious enough to necessitate the firemen remaining almost until dawn to check that it did not start up again. When Vanessa went to view the manor just as dawn was breaking her heart was in her mouth, but outwardly nothing had changed.

'Most of the damage inside is just smoke.' Gavin told her when she offered him the flask of coffee she had brought. 'Jay is getting his architect down to have a look at it. Apparently they start on the modernisation next week—you needn't look like that,' he told his sister, 'Jay wants the place restoring, more or less to what it was.'

'So you see, I'm not quite the philistine you imagined.' Jay's voice came, light and dry behind her. Like Gavin he was covered in smuts, his face and hands practically black, his eyes blank with exhaustion. Lines she had not noticed before added a carved harshness to his face, showing her what he would be like in later life. Her heart ached with love and compassion for him. She longed to take him in her arms, to comfort him, and ease the frown from between his eyes.

'I've told Jay he can come back with us. He might as well try to get a few hours' sleep. That's okay isn't it?'

Okay! Vanessa daren't look at Jay. 'It's fine,' she assured her brother in a calm voice. She had never imagined she possessed any acting talent at all, but she was fast coming to realise she had been wrong.

'I'll go back now and make up the spare bed.'

'Yes, and you'd better make sure there's plenty

of hot water,' Gavin called after her. 'We're both going to need it.'

It was just over an hour later when she heard Jay's car pull up outside. The lodge had five bedrooms, but Vanessa had chosen the one which had always been dubbed the 'guest' room for Jay, because it was the only one with its own bathroom. Coffee was perking in the kitchen as they walked in the door, and Gavin sniffed the aromatic scent of it appreciatively, throwing down the leather jerkin he had been wearing, careless of the ring of soot it left on the pristine floor.

'Gavin.' Vanessa bent to retrieve it automatically, taking it outside to shake it. When she came back Jay was watching her with a frown, his eyes wary, gold and black, making little tremors of apprehension flicker along her spine.

'Very domesticated,' he drawled dryly as Vanessa picked up a cloth to mop up the dust.

Gavin glanced at him in surprise. 'Oh yes V . . .' Just in time he caught back her name and supplemented, 'Very domesticated is our Nadia. Quite the little housewife. The man who gets her is getting a real treasure. Cooks like a dream too . . .'

She could almost see the withdrawal in Jay's face. Did Gavin realise what he was doing, she wondered angrily. He was practically trying to sell her virtues to Jay, at least that was the way it sounded. After she had shown Jay to the guest room, merely opening the door, and then leaving quickly before he could accuse her of deliberately promoting any intimacy between them, she went back down to the kitchen.

'Honestly Gavin,' she complained, 'did you have

to sound quite so much as though you couldn't wait to see me married? As though I am touting for a husband in fact?'

'Sorry about that,' he looked sheepish. 'The fact is, when I nearly blurted your name out, it threw me so much that I just gabbled out the first thing that came into my head. Anyway Jay's much too sensible to think anything like that?'

'Is he?' Vanessa wondered if she should tell her brother the truth and then dismissed the idea. It would only make the whole situation more complicated. Where originally she had longed for her brief deception to be over, now she dreaded its ending, because with it would come the ending of their affair.

'I'm going up to bed now,' Gavin told her. 'You look tired too. Why don't you try and snatch a few hours as well. You must be as exhausted as we are.'

She *was* tired, and Gavin's suggestion seemed a sensible one. Even so, it was hard not to think of Jay lying in bed in the same house not three doors away, perhaps even wanting her as much as she wanted him. Sighing Vanessa turned on her side and tried to court sleep. She couldn't go to Jay and he obviously wasn't going to come to her. So far their relationship seemed to be a series of interrupted events. The aching in the pit of her stomach re-ignited as she remembered his caresses. Her body trembled, and when she did sleep it was to dream of dark gold eyes, and Jay's hands touching her body transporting her to a place where they could always be together.

When she woke up she felt totally disorientated.

The sky was a rich deep blue. In the distance she could just about see the rooftops of the manor, miraculously barely damaged. Last night Jay had shown her beyond any shadow of a doubt how much he wanted her, so why should she have this feeling of unease, this conviction that Nemesis was waiting in the shadows to deal her some unimaginable blow? Guilty conscience, she told herself as she pulled on her robe and opened her bedroom door. The door to Jay's room stood open; the bed empty. Her apprehension fluttered and grew becoming fully-fledged alarm.

In the bathroom she showered quickly, brushing her teeth, examining the faint bruise marks on her skin and flushing as she remembered how they had got there. Everything was all wrong. She ought to have been waking up this morning feeling fulfilled as a woman only can be after a night spent in her lover's arms. Instead she felt very guilty, very uncertain, and most definitely not fulfilled.

The kitchen was empty; someone had been down and made coffee because the percolator was still on and half full, and there was a loaf of bread on the table, perhaps Gavin and Jay were up and had gone out? She went outside and discovered that Jay's car had gone. A sharp stab of disappointment shot through her. Couldn't he at least have waited to say goodbye? She was being childish, she told herself. She had no reason at all to feel so deserted, so abandoned. Doubtless Jay had a thousand and one things to do, and he and Gavin had sensibly decided to leave her sleeping.

But when she went back in the kitchen she realised that wherever Jay had gone he had gone alone, because Gavin was standing there, still wearing his pyjamas, scratching his chest reflectively, his hair tousled, and his face unshaven.

'Any coffee going?' he asked sleepily. 'I'm dying for a cup. Any sign of Jay by the way?'

'He's gone,' Vanessa told him quietly. 'I've only just got up myself, so I don't know when or where. I suppose he's got a lot to do.'

'Umm. I expect so. By the way, did you hear someone knocking on the door earlier. God knows what time it was. What time is it now by the way?'

'Half twelve,' Vanessa told him. 'And no I didn't hear anyone. Perhaps it was the milkman, I didn't pay him last week.'

'Could be. I want to go up to the manor today and take some pictures. I've developed the ones we took yesterday. Want to see them?'

Vanessa nodded unenthusiastically. The last thing she wanted right now was to be reminded of that scene in the changing rooms. She was just pouring the coffee when she heard Gavin coming back, whistling as he walked into the kitchen, a large grin on his face.

'Come and have a look.' Before Vanessa could protest, he made a large space for himself on the kitchen table and spread out the prints. Vanessa approached them nervously, moistening her lips. She had always hated having her photograph taken knowing it would give people even more opportunity to compare her unfavourably with Nadia—Nadia whose sexuality came across so provocatively in her photographs, Nadia who shared her features but of whom she was somehow a pale, insignificant shadow.

'Come on, look, they aren't as bad as all that!' Gavin instructed her. She glanced at them, her eyes widening slightly as she moved closer for a better look. 'See what I mean?' Gavin asked slyly. 'Seems to me that a few mistakes have been made around here. Nadia's photogenic all right, primarily because she makes love to the camera, but you're something else. Look at these cheekbones . . . these eyes . . .' Growing more and more enthusiastic, Gavin traced the features that were so familiar to her and yet which the camera seemed to have captured with an elusive something she couldn't recognise. The girl staring back at her from the photographs had her face, and yet there was something else something undefinable that made her someone you wanted to look at and then look at again.

'I should have done this years ago,' Gavin told her seriously, 'but you were always so damned determined not to let me. Unlike Nadia . . . I know you've always thought of yourself as inferior to her, as second best, but these ought to prove conclusively to you once and for all that you've got something she hasn't. Nadia's a taker Van, she could drain a man dry and then throw him on one side. You're a giver, and it shows. Here . . .' he touched her mouth, 'and here.' He smiled into her eyes. 'I think Jay's going to be very pleased with these. Speaking of whom, isn't that his car I hear?'

Vanessa's ears caught the distinctive purr of Jay's expensive sports car, her heart suddenly constricting, her throat muscles ridging tight with apprehension and excitement. He had come back. Heavens, she was like an adolescent deep in the throes of her first impossible love. But then there wasn't all that much difference, except that she ought to be old enough to know better, she warned herself sardonically. He was her first love, and it was definitely an impossible one.

The car engine had stopped. She heard the sound of a door slamming and her heart thudding an excited beat, Gavin had gone to open the door, and suddenly, so suddenly that her heart seemed to plummet downwards in a never-ending jolting ride, Gavin said hoarsely, 'Oh my God, no. Vanessa...' She moved towards the door, in obedience to the command in his voice, standing as though she had been turned to stone as Jay opened the passenger door of his car, and helped his passenger to alight. Vanessa didn't need to spend much time looking at her, one briefly comprehensive glance was enough! It was Nadia!

The couple approached the door together, a fact with a significance which did not escape Vanessa. She felt cold, cold right through to her bones, and any hopes she might have had that there was still a chance to extricate herself from the situation and salvage her relationship with Jay were dashed the moment she saw Nadia's face. On it was the expression of malicious triumph she knew so well, her cousin's hand resting possessively on Jay's bare forearm, her nails dark red, the colour of blood as they stroked his bare skin. Jay had changed. He was wearing cream coloured jeans and a dark blue shirt, and her mind tormented her with images of Nadia with him in his bedroom, helping him to undress ... touching him ... Nausea welled up inside her, turning her skin so pale that Gavin thought she was going to faint.

'Well darlings, what *have* you been up to,' Nadia purred, adding in that husky, seductive voice she always adopted when she was about to be particularly unkind—the scorpion before it stung—'Be sure thy sins will find thee out, wasn't that what they always used to tell us at Sunday School? Vanessa you naughty girl what *have* you been doing? I could be very angry with both of you, but I think I understand how it was. I don't suppose you could resist could you darling?' Her smile was saccharine sweet, and much as she longed to avoid Jay's eyes Vanessa forced herself to meet them. The look in them confirmed all her worst fears. He was looking right through her, looking at her as though she simply did not exist. Something started to break apart inside her, her body seemed to be weeping tears of anguish killing her slowly inside.

'Nadia, what are *you* doing here?' Gavin interrupted angrily. Dark pencilled eyebrows rose, the full round lips forming a soft moue. As always her make-up was immaculate, her clothes expensive emphasising her willowy figure. 'Darling I should have thought it was obvious, or haven't you seen the morning papers.' There was one on the table, and Gavin picked it up flicking through it in grim silence, pausing suddenly to study something before showing it to Vanessa. It was a gossip column item, a report that the latest girlfriend of millionaire businessman Jay Courtland was the beautiful model Nadia March whom he had met in her home town of Clarewell.

'Naturally I was curious,' Nadia told them, her eyes hardening as they rested on Vanessa's pale countenance. 'I hardly need ask why you did it, need I darling? I suppose you thought with me out of the country that you'd never be found out?' Her full lips curved cynically. 'Unfortunately for you the job finished sooner than we expected.' She looked from Vanessa's pale face to Jay's remote one. 'I'm a little bit cross with you too Jay. How could you mistake Vanessa for *me*? How amusing. I suppose my frigid little cousin was using my name and personality to help her find out what it means to be made love to by a real man. Darling Van always did have trouble in that direction,' she added maliciously, fixing beautifully made up sapphire eyes on Vanessa. 'Do you remember darling, every time you got a boyfriend they always seemed to prefer me ... Of course you mustn't blame Van, Jay,' she cooed turning to the man at her side. 'She's always had this dreadful chip on her shoulder where I'm concerned; always been so jealous of me. Even as a child people used to remark on it. After all it's hardly my fault that I'm more attractive. We both look alike, but Vanessa has always been in my shadow.' She pouted again. 'I suppose she looked on you as her last chance to find out what life's all about; a chance to free herself from her repressed virgin image. Or were you trying to be cleverer than that darling?' she asked detaching her gaze to look at Vanessa, her eyes as cold and hard as ice. 'Were you going to let Jay take you to bed and then cry rape hoping he'd do the gentlemanly thing and marry you?' A trill of silvery laughter floated into the thick silence of the kitchen. Vanessa felt numb; too battered from the brutality of Vanessa's barbs to fight back.

How could her cousin behave like this, and in front of a stranger, but then Nadia had never lost an opportunity to belittle her. She shivered suddenly glad of Gavin's protective arm round her shoulders.

'Stop talking to Van like that Nadia,' he told her curtly. 'You've got it all wrong. Jay mistook Vanessa for you, and then when he wanted her to pose with the team, I asked her to keep up the deception ... Vanessa is in no way to blame ...'

'No? You always did spring to her defence didn't you? But this time your precious little sister isn't as innocent as you think. At least I don't consider it innocent to go to bed with a man knowing he thinks you're someone else. Something, darling,' she purred, turning to Jay, 'that I'll make sure isn't likely to happen again. Once you've known the real thing, you aren't likely to confuse me with my drab little cousin ever again. How unfortunate for you darlings, that Jay should have been the one to open the door to me this morning.' Her eyes mocked Vanessa. 'I found his method of introducing himself most unusual ... especially when he seemed to think we'd shared more than merely kisses already ...'

Vanessa felt acutely sick picturing the scene. Nadia's arrival, Jay, thinking it was her, taking her in his arms, kissing her ... discovering ... her stomach revolted, nausea lurching through her.

Jay hadn't spoken a word throughout the entire scene, but now Vanessa couldn't prevent herself from turning towards him, from begging him with her eyes to understand, to let her explain, but all he said was, 'Nadia, if you're ready to leave ...'

'Jay?' Her voice was a husky cry of protest, halting him as he was about to stoop through the door. 'Please ... I can explain ...'

'There's nothing *to* explain,' he told her harshly. 'Nadia is right. You're just jealous of her Vanessa, jealous and so insecure that you had to steal her identity.'

'*I* was the one you held in your arms,' Vanessa told him in tortured accents, driven to an open pleading she could never have envisioned.

'Yes, but only because I thought you were Nadia,' Jay told her cruelly. 'Nadia was the one I wanted to make love to Vanessa, not you. I'll speak to you later,' he told Gavin abruptly. 'We'll have to set up another photographic session—this time using the right model. Nadia has agreed.' He turned to Vanessa one last time his eyes hard, yellow as a tiger's, flat and unforgiving. 'If there's one thing I detest it's dishonesty, and I think you're the most cravenly dishonest person I've ever met. Now that I've seen you together, I think I must have been blind. You're very much the dross aren't you Vanessa?' he said with deliberate cruelty as he stepped through the door. 'Very much a pale imitation of the real thing.'

Dimly she heard Gavin swearing as the car revved up, distantly she was aware of his arms going round her, of him carrying her upstairs and placing her on her bed. She knew he was talking to her, apologising, blaming himself for what had happened, calling Nadia a malicious bitch, but none of it seemed to matter. She had retreated inside herself to a place where nothing could reach her, a place where there was no pain, no feeling at all, only Jay's last words, falling through her mind like stones dropped in a deep pond, and if she let them keep on falling they might disappear into the mud and remain buried there so that she need never hear them again.

CHAPTER SIX

A HOLIDAY away was what the doctor recommended. He had known her since childhood, and was tactful enough not to ask too many probing questions. Nervous strain was his diagnosis, and Vanessa numbly accepted Gavin's decision that a holiday would do her good. She was to go to Spain and spend a fortnight there with friends of Gavin's who owned a villa. She had neither objected nor commented when he told her. She felt completely indifferent to everything; like a stuffed doll. Somewhere deep inside her was pain, chained up like a dangerous animal just waiting to snap its chains and tear her to pieces, so she mustn't move, she mustn't think, in case, accidentally, she set it free.

Sue and David Carling were a pleasant couple in their mid thirties with two sons of ten and eight. The villa was a comfortable one on a luxurious development and while they were happy to include Vanessa in all their activities they did not push her into joining them.

She spent the first three days alone in the small cove just beyond the development, far enough away, over a difficult headland path to make it too much of an effort for the other holidaymakers to get there. There was nothing in the bay, no houses, or bars, simply the curving protection of the cliffs and the soft white sand. Slowly like someone waking from a dream she forced herself to remember, to recall what had happened, making herself relive every painful second. At first she kept wanting to escape, to let her mind drift to other things, but gradually her control grew stronger; she could go through that final scene, if not without flinching then at least without escaping cowardly into other things; other times. The only thing she could not do was think about Jay making love to her. As yet she did not have the defences to face that, and perhaps never would. How much truth had there been in the accusations he and Nadia had flung at her with such scorn? She forced herself to face the possibility that there could be some. She was no less sparing with herself than they had been, knowing she had come to a crossroads in her life. She loved Jay, that couldn't be altered, ignored or obliterated, but there were still choices she had to make, between passive acceptance of her misery or a constructive attempt to take what was left to her and build on it. Her pride, what shattered remnants of it were left would not allow her to degenerate into the object of everyone's pity. Knowing Nadia, there could not be any of their friends who didn't know the full story now. She had to return to Clarewell, her home and her work were there, but never, ever again was she going to play second-best, from now on she was herself; and people must accept and want her as herself not as a substitute for Nadia.

The decision once made seemed to release some of her numbness. There was pain to be faced, agonising pain that brought her back from her sojourns on the beach white-faced and drawn, but at least she was facing up to it.

'I know you're going through a bad time,' Sue commented quietly on the third evening. 'If you want to talk about it, I'm always here, and I promise you it won't go any further—not even to Dave.'

Vanessa believed her. 'Did Gavin tell you anything?'

'Only that you'd had a very bad experience which was mainly his fault. He's very worried about you Vanessa. Very worried.'

'I know.'

It was the end of the week before she could bring herself to talk to Sue and only then because she knew that talking to someone else was the best way to come to terms with the wreckage of her life.

Dave had taken the boys into town, and she and Sue were alone by the pool. She told her what had happened as simply and emotionlessly as she could, and then waited.

'Phew, that cousin of yours sounds a first-rate bitch!' was Sue's initial comment. 'You do get them you know,' she added when she saw Vanessa's uncertain face. 'Oh I know you've obviously been brought up to think she's the best thing since sliced bread, and she's obviously made capital out of it but she strikes me as one very egotistical, self-centred young lady—a true product of the 'Me' generation. You know Vanessa,' she added thoughtfully, 'I shouldn't be surprised if she isn't envious of you.' She saw Vanessa's expression, and said, 'Oh yes, I'm perfectly serious. There are people like that you know who want it all, who can't bear anyone else to have anything. Possibly the reason she's worked so hard at keeping you down is because she fears that really you could eclipse her, but that doesn't help you with Jay Courtland. I'm not going to hand out any false platitudes. From what you tell me about him I get the impression he's the sort of man who simply doesn't want commitments cluttering up his life. A loner and perhaps a little bitter, certainly very wary of our sex; and of any member of it who comes anywhere near breaching his defences. You won't like what I'm going to say next Van, but it has to be said,' she added gently. 'Even these days, we're most of us brought up to believe in the potency of true love; of good over evil and happy ever afters. If I ever have a daughter I'm going to tell her how it really is believe me. Don't waste your life in vain hopes. He laid his cards on the table for you from what you've said. He wanted the kind of uninvolved purely sexual relationship he can have with the Nadias of this world. Even if you'd been prepared to settle for an affair I think he'd have shied off from the emotional commitment you would have demanded. Some men are like that, and I'm afraid that you're just going to have to accept that that's the way it is. I know how badly it must hurt, but I think you're just going to have to accept that in his mind you were always Nadia and that he's more likely to transfer whatever desire he felt for you to her, than to pursue a relationship with you.'

It was exactly what she had felt herself and at

least it had the virtue of cutting clean, even though she felt she would die from the pain in her heart. 'Don't go on hoping,' Sue told her gently, covering her hand with her own, 'there's a very true saying that goes, "Hope too long defereth maketh the heart grow sick." I should hate to see that happen to you.'

The next morning she rang Gavin. He sounded pleased to hear from her, and told her rather hesitantly that Jay hadn't withdrawn the contract. 'If you don't feel like coming back here just yet I'll understand,' he told her, his voice distorted and faint on the continental line.

'I can't run away for ever Gavin,' she responded. 'I've got to face it sometime. The sooner I do, the sooner I can put the whole thing behind me.' She didn't ask about Jay or Nadia and Gavin didn't mention them, and yet once she had replaced the receiver, her desire to know where Jay was and what he was doing burned into her like a fever, like a craving for water in the heat of the desert.

She spent what was left of the morning on the more public beach near the villas. She had taken her camera with her and began idly to use it, snapping two dark, obviously very Spanish and correct small boys as they played by the shore. One of them ran into the sea hotly pursued by the other, but as Vanessa watched the smaller child lost his balance and disappeared beneath the surface. The water was barely a foot deep, but Vanessa acted instinctively, relieved that she had done so as she picked the choking child out of the water, patting him automatically on the back. His choking cries attracted attention and within minutes a tall dark-haired man was at her side, his Spanish soft and rapid, until she shook her head and said hesitantly, 'Sorry I'm English.'

'Ah English! A race noted for its phlegm, is that not so? But I shouldn't tease you señorita, Carlos here has good reason to be thankful for your prompt action. I doubt that my sister will entrust me with the care of her *pequeños* again once she hears the tale of this morning's mishap.'

'Yes, it's frightening how easily children get into trouble, one minute they're there and the next . . .'

'Yes, and these two seem to be experts at disappearing.'

Still carrying Carlos who refused to be parted from her she walked with him back to where the children's things lay on the sand close to her own towel and camera. As he took Carlos from her he introduced himself, 'Roberto Mendoza, and these two are my nephews, Carlos and Felipe. Forgive me if this sounds rather trite, but I feel sure that I have seen you somewhere before.' His forehead wrinkled as though he was striving to remember where. 'Believe me I am not just saying this, handing a line, I believe you call it in your language. Your face is very familiar to me and yet I cannot think why. I only arrived in San Felipe this morning . . .'

'It could be that you are confusing me with my cousin, she's a model,' Vanessa heard herself saying quite calmly, 'We look very alike, physically that is . . .'

'I cannot believe Heaven would be cruel enough to torment mortal man by creating two such beautiful women,' Roberto protested flattering her with his eyes, 'Nor can I believe that this cousin you speak of could be as beautiful as you *nia* . . .'

He was flattering her outrageously, and suddenly it didn't matter any more that she was Vanessa and not Nadia, at least not here. She was herself, and a very attractive, very male Spaniard was making it quite plain that he was enjoying her company. Carlos had recovered from his ordeal, and having accepted his offer to buy her a cup of coffee Vanessa accompanied Roberto and the two children to a nearby café, where they talked for well over an hour before Vanessa realised that practically for the first time in her life she had not been worried about her ability to hold another person's attention, nor had she been looking constantly over her shoulder, waiting for the overpowering shadow of her cousin to pounce. Suddenly she felt completely free of the inferiority complex which had haunted her youth, and when Roberto asked her out to dinner she accepted almost instantly.

During the second week of their holiday Sue teased Vanessa about Roberto's very obvious preference for her company. 'He owns a company which builds holidays homes like these,' she told her. 'He is extremely eligible, unmarried, rich . . .' she glanced coyly at Vanessa, 'and you seem to like him.'

'"Like" being the operative word,' Vanessa agreed with a smile. Being with Roberto after being with Jay was like drinking flat lemonade after a surfeit of champagne; the only thing the two had in common was that both could quench one's thirst. It was very pleasant to flirt with Roberto and enjoy his lazy flattery. He wasn't serious about her, any more than she was about him. He had kissed her once or twice, light, teasing kisses, which he had had the intuition to take no further, when he realised how half-hearted her response was.

'Ah, you are an old-fashioned girl who intends to keep that passion one senses so tantalisingly, locked away for the man who will be your husband and your lover is that it?'

His words gave her heart a painful jerk, but she kept her voice even as she replied, 'I'm afraid so.'

'But we can still be friends you and I,' Roberto said gently, 'I like talking to you Vanessa March, I like the quickness of your mind and the compassion of your heart. The man who wins your love will be fortunate indeed, there is so much treasure there for him. I have seen pictures of this cousin of yours now in my sister's magazines. You are wrong, you are not at all alike,' he said positively. 'Her eyes lack your innocence; they are hard and cold, her beauty that of a mask someone might don to hide the truth. Your beauty is of the soul as well as the face. To compare yourself to her is like comparing spring water to salt water— both might look the same, but one gives life and the other takes it. No one with the eyes to see, could ever mistake you for your cousin, *niña*.'

He wanted her to stay on after her holiday was over. She had told him a good deal about herself, and he had suggested that there might be a job for her with his organisation, doing photographic layouts of the villas his company rented out as holiday homes, and those he sold as permanent homes. 'Think about it,' he urged her on their last night together. 'You have not told me about it, but I can see there is some unhappiness in your life. Here in Spain the warmth of our sun will melt the coldness from your heart.'

'By running away?' she asked wryly, 'No Roberto, I must go home.'

But not with any false hopes in her heart, or any chance of deceiving herself. What had been between Jay and herself was gone, dead, finished with. The Vanessa returning to Clarewell was not the Vanessa who left in such a dull fog of despair that she had been conscious of nothing except the battle to overcome her own pain. She parted from Sue and David at the airport, having thanked them for their company and their understanding. 'Any time,' Sue grinned. 'You've got our address. We'd love you to come and stay, I've got a cousin who goes mad for black-haired blue eyed females. I can't wait to see the effect you have on him. I had the most almighty crush on him twenty years ago, and I can't wait to see him get his come-uppance.' It was all very lighthearted and designed to boost her ego, but she didn't need the crutches of other people's compassion now. She accepted who and what she was; that she would never be Nadia and also that she never need stand in her cousin's shadow again. She was her own person, with her own personality.

She could tell that Gavin sensed the change in her the moment she stepped off the train. She had bought new clothes in Seville, expensive, but discreet clothes that banished for ever the girl who had hidden her body in jeans and baggy shirts. Her hair had been trimmed and re-shaped into a flattering bell, and she had learned by watching Sue and Roberto's sister, the art of applying make-up to subtly emphasise her beauty, rather than as the highly sophisticated mask adopted by Nadia. She no longer felt ashamed of her own curves in comparison to Nadia's greyhound sleekness. Roberto had often glanced admiringly at her figure when he thought she wasn't looking. She had taken a leaf from the Spanish women's book, and had chosen clothes in rich colours, a perfect foil for her black hair and pale skin. Deep shades of rose and blue; fabrics in silks, soft wools and linens attractive to the touch, subtly provocative without the outright sexyness of the clothes Nadia favoured. In two weeks she had done a surprising amount of assessing and self analysing and had come to understand that in her determination to be as different from Nadia as possible she had crushed a vital part of herself, denying her basic femininity because she had dreaded people thinking she was copying her cousin.

Gavin's sidelong looks told her how much he liked the change in her, and a teasing smile curved her mouth when he eventually said with brotherly candour. 'You've changed Van, grown up ... I don't know what,' he shook his head wonderingly. 'You've got one hell of a lot more poise than you had when you left. Nadia had better watch out, from now on I think you're going to be more competition than she can safely handle. She's going to blow her top. She's always been used to being top dog, but she's forgotten that a pretty face without the personality to go with it is like wrapping an empty box in glittering paper. The moment the paper comes off—disenchantment.'

'I haven't changed that much. Just done some long overdue thinking, and I certainly don't intend going into competition with Nadia—for anything.'

'From what I heard you don't need to. What's this Sue tells me about some handsome young Spaniard?'

They were both laughing when he brought the Volvo to a halt outside the studio. When Vanessa looked surprised, Gavin said gravely, 'There's something I have to show you before we go home.'

She followed him upstairs in silence. 'Have a look at these,' he instructed her, handing her a batch of photographs. 'Jay told me to take them just after you left.'

She had known almost instinctively what she would see, but that didn't stop the jolt of pain, like catching the exposed nerve of a tooth, knowing it would hurt and yet not able to stop probing.

The photographs all featured her cousin, posing as Vanessa had done in the 'tub' at the football team's grounds—with one eye-catching difference. Nadia was posing as Vanessa had refused to do, the upper half of her body completely nude, her pose one of almost preening, purring satisfaction as though she enjoyed being the cynosure of so many male eyes.

'It was on the cards,' Vanessa said quietly, 'At least Jay got what he wanted. I'm glad it all worked out okay and that you didn't lose the contract.'

'No, I thought we would, but Jay said he didn't

have the time to waste looking for someone else, and besides he admitted that he liked our work. I told him that I was the one to blame, Van.' He fiddled awkwardly with the prints as he picked them up. 'I didn't realise you'd fallen for him. I didn't have him tagged as your type . . .'

'He isn't,' Vanessa agreed. 'I think Nadia was right, I let the fact that I was playing her go to my head, and went in right over it, but I'm okay now.'

'That was some scene in the kitchen that morning. Trust Nadia to make the most of it. She and Jay seem a pretty hot item at the moment.'

'Hardly surprising.' Really it was amazing how easy it was to keep the pain at bay. All she had to do was to conjure the magic word 'dross' and the sound of Jay's voice when he uttered it. It had all the potency of a black magic charm. 'Any work for me to do?' she asked brightly,

Gavin took his tone from her, putting the prints away and disappearing into his office, returning with a thick folder. 'Now that you mention it— plenty. Jay wants full photographic coverage of the team when the season starts—and before, and the architect working on the manor wants detailed photographs taken as they work. Jay wants you to work with the team. I'll do the house!'

Her heart thudded slowly. Careful, she warned herself. That frail feeling flowering inside her came dangerously close to hope—something she thought she had extinguished in the long, lonely reaches of the night when she battled against her feelings for him and thought them subdued.

'Oh?' She forced her face to show nothing of her inner turmoil. 'Why? A grand gesture of mag-

nanimity? A consolation prize for the loser?' Or
something more subtle and infinitely more cruel
her mind asked. She had his measure now. No
commitments, and he was ruthless enough to
reinforce that over and over again until he was
sure it was understood, whatever the cost in pain
and humiliation to herself.

'Perhaps because he recognises that you're a
first-rate photographer.,' Gavin said watching her.
'I can't force you to do it Van.'

'Of course not, and besides there's no need. My
education has been badly neglected, I don't know
the first thing about football—I think I'm going to
enjoy the next few months.' She smiled at her
brother, amazed by her own capacity for duplicity.
She wasn't going to enjoy them at all, and Jay
Courtland, damn him, was probably counting on
that very fact. He didn't want her. Fine! She
wasn't going to inflict herself on him like some
moony, star-struck teenager.

'When do I start?' she asked Gavin cheerfully.

'I'm having dinner with Jay tonight, I'll ask him
then. I told him you were coming home today.'

'And of course, he didn't extend his invitation
to include me. Hardly to be expected after all. Tell
him I'm ready to start work whenever he wants me
to, Gavin. I think I'll have an early night tonight
anyway.'

In the event she didn't. Just after Gavin went
out the phone rang. When she picked up the
receiver, an unfamiliar voice spoke her name.

'Yes, this is she,' she murmured, wondering
about the identity of her caller.

'You probably won't remember me,' the

unfamiliar male voice told her, 'but we have met. At the football club, I'm Jeff Marsden, one of the players.'

Jeff Marsden! She did remember vaguely. The longest serving member of the team, he was something of a local pin-up. Tall, ruggedly goodlooking with fair hair and laughing blue eyes. Ten years older than her, Vanessa remembered he had been at the same school, although several years before her.

'Jeff, yes of course I remember you!' The new confidence she had gained in Spain came through in her voice, and she could almost feel him do a double take. 'Hey, that sounds promisingly flattering. I rang to ask if there was any chance of taking you out to dinner tonight. I've called a couple of times recently, but you never seem to be in.'

'I've only just got back from Spain,' Vanessa told him, 'and yes, I'd love to go out.' She had to start re-entering the world again some time. It wasn't retaliation against Jay or anything so foolish, or infantile. Jay didn't want her in his life. She had forced herself to accept that, and now she must build a fresh life for herself from the ruins, somehow she must learn how to fill the yawning emptiness inside herself, not by flinging herself into a series of cheap affairs, not by sacrificing her self-respect to disprove the cutting jeers Nadia had flung to her, but by making friends, accepting whatever life chose to offer her instead of running away from it.

'Hey that's great. Where would you like to go?'

'Somewhere where I can show off my new tan?' Vanessa teased, suddenly feeling light-hearted.

'It will be my pleasure,' Jeff responded gallantly, 'I'll be round in about an hour if that's okay with you?'

She was just putting the finishing touches to her make-up when she heard him arrive, and was downstairs to open the door to him by the time he had stopped his car.

'Wow!' he whistled appreciatively as he stepped into the hall. 'I'm the one who'll be doing the showing off!' His eyes, entirely male, and extremely admiring studied her vibrant appearance. Her dark hair was piled on top of her head and secured with the very pretty mother of pearl combs Roberto had insisted on giving her before she left Spain. Her dress was a rich deep crimson, fine layers of silk with tiny shoe string straps and a discreetly provocative bodice, its circular skirt swishing flatteringly against her legs when she moved. High heeled crimson sandals and a white shawl completed her outfit, the scent of her perfume clinging to her skin as she followed Jeff out to his car. His manner—so awed and almost deferential amused her, and she found as they drove through the countryside that she was quite relaxed, and was soon drawing him out, asking him about his life, and when he had decided to build it around the game of football.

'It actually chose me,' he admitted as he turned his head to glance at her profile. Funny how people had always thought her the dull, plain cousin, looking at her tonight . . .

'Eyes back on the road,' Vanessa chided him teasingly, 'Go on, you were saying . . .'

'Oh yes, I played for the school team and was

picked out by a local talent scout. By that time I knew that I wasn't going to make it to university so when I was offered a chance to play for the second team I leapt at it, and that's about it. I doubt that Courtland will keep me on much longer. I'm past my best, which reached its peak when I played for England. Now I'm a good solid reserve, but not really first team material.'

'You sound remarkably unconcerned.'

She saw him shrug. 'Well I've seen it coming. I've invested the money I've earned—my brother and I are partners in a small garden centre, and there's plenty of work waiting for me there when I leave the team. I've had a good innings, it's time I gave someone else the chance . . . although I must say I'd like a final good season.'

'M . . .' Vanessa was deep in thought. An idea had occurred to her, but she wanted to talk it over with Gavin before she took it any further. She thought the publicity for the team would have a more general appeal if it contained some details of the players' outside lives; what their hopes and ambitions were, what they did when they weren't playing football. It would help to make them come alive for those whose lives were not bound up in the game.

She came to with a start as the car lost speed and she saw the dark bulk of a building looming up in front of her. Her heart stopped and then started to thud jerkily as she recognised the outline of the waterwheel. Of all the places Jeff had to bring her, what had made him choose here?

'I wasn't sure if you'd been here before, but it's very popular,' he told her as he parked the car.

'You did stipulate somewhere where you could show off, and on Thursdays they always have dancing here later on. It's very popular and very well attended.'

'So well attended that you were able to get us a table at the last minute?' Vanessa mocked, lifting one eyebrow.

Jeff grinned in pleased response. 'Ah, you noticed, that's the fabled Marsden charm!'

'I think now is the time to warn you that charm is something I'm generally immune to,' Vanessa told him gently. She was enjoying his company, but she didn't want him to get any false ideas.

'I thought it might be. I've always liked discerning females,' he added.

'Oh.' Her eyes were innocently amused. 'What makes you think I am?'

'I'm sure of it,' he said softly, 'After all you agreed to come out with me didn't you? I'm sure in no time at all you'll have seen through the face I show to the world and discovered the intensely charismatic, and yet humble character I really am.'

They were both laughing when they entered the restaurant, and Vanessa barely noticed the interested and appreciative looks they attracted as they were shown to their table. The waiter seated them and then produced the menus with a flourish. It was obvious that Jeff was a well known diner, and it was very pleasant to sit and bask in the glow of his admiration. She gave the waiter her order unselfconsciously and then settled back to wait for her food, her attention suddenly caught by someone familiar glimpsed out of the corner of her eye. As she turned her head she saw her brother seated several tables away, deep in conversation with Jay Courtland, Nadia preening herself at his side.

It was as bad as she had expected, but surely nothing she wasn't prepared for she thought pragmatically, as Nadia lifted her head and saw her, contempt giving way to surprise as Vanessa returned her scrutiny with cool amusement. Nadia's eyes were the first to drop, a faint flush of something that could have been anger, colouring her cheekbones. Her cousin looked too thin Vanessa thought studying her; and why had she never noticed before that petulant droop to her mouth, and those tiny lines of dissatisfaction radiating out from her eyes?

The wine waiter arrived, and to her surprise he was opening a bottle of champagne. Jeff laughed when he saw her bemused expression. 'What are we celebrating?' she asked him.

'I'm celebrating the fact that you agreed to have dinner with me,' he told her teasingly, 'of course you can join me, but if you do I'll take it as a sign that you're celebrating because I asked you.'

Six weeks ago she would have been tongue-tied, now she just laughed, raising her glass to his and savouring the sharp, bubbling liquid. That was when Jay looked across and saw them. Their eyes met and locked, cold dislike in his, cool dismissal in hers. She could almost feel him registering the shock. Good, she thought watching him. You told me once you didn't want me Mr Courtland, I got the message, you'll never need to tell me again.

CHAPTER SEVEN

IT was inevitable after they had finished eating that Gavin should come over and talk to them. 'Van,' he exclaimed, obviously puzzled. 'I thought you were having an early night.'

Without turning her head Vanessa knew that Jay was watching them. What had he expected, she wondered bitterly; that she would become a hermit simply because *he* had rejected her? The thought fuelled her determination lending a smoky warmth to her voice as she said huskily while smiling at Jeff, 'Someone made me an offer I couldn't refuse.' Briefly she introduced the two men, listening to them exchanging pleasantries, all the time intensely aware of Jay's silent scrutiny.

'Nadia's seething,' Gavin told her with a grin, breaking through her thoughts. 'You've quite stolen her thunder.' When she looked bemused he explained. 'She came here tonight expecting to be the centre of attention, but all eyes seem to be on you. I like that dress, is it new?'

'I bought it in Spain,' Vanessa told him casually, adding wryly, 'There's no need to over do the partisanship Gavin. I'm all grown up now and don't have the slightest desire to compete with Nadia.'

'If you'll allow me to say so, the boot is very much on the other foot,' Jeff interrupted watching her speculatively. 'Just take a look around you if

121

you don't believe me. You've been attracting a considerable amount of male attention ever since we walked in. I was hoping you'd never notice,' he added with a grin. 'I don't think I can stand the competition.'

Something in his smile told Vanessa that he wasn't exaggerating or flattering her, but strangely enough the knowledge that she had stolen the limelight from Nadia gave her no satisfaction at all. There was the same hollow emptiness there had been ever since Jay rejected her.

Gavin returned to his own table and Jeff asked her to dance. She accepted, liking the way he made no attempt to hold her too closely when the music switched to a more romantic number. He was an amusing and pleasant companion, who didn't make demands on her that she wasn't able to meet, yet despite her apparent total concentration on him, she knew the exact second when Jay left the restaurant; she could sense it in the easing of the hot pressure on the back of her neck where she had felt the intense heat of his glance searing her skin as she and Jeff danced.

It was quite late when they left the restaurant. As Jeff brought his car to a halt outside the lodge Vanessa could see lights glimmering at the manor. Was Jay there with Nadia? An agonising pang of jealousy tore through her carefully erected defences as she ruthlessly tried to banish the mental image tormenting her. Nadia in Jay's arms; Jay kissing and caressing her cousin, sharing with her the pleasures he had denied her.

'Vanessa?'

She realised that Jeff had been saying something

and gave him an apologetic smile. 'Sorry, I still haven't completely re-adjusted to the time difference.'

'I was asking if you would come out with me again? Not this week because we start the pre-season training, but perhaps next?'

'I'd like that,' Vanessa told him, accepting the tentative pressure of his mouth against hers, willing herself not to compare her reaction to Jeff's kiss as opposed to Jay's, and then gently disentangling herself before he could deepen the embrace.

Gavin was just making himself a cup of coffee when she walked into the kitchen.

'Hello there. All alone?' he asked casually, adding when she nodded her head. 'Quite a surprise seeing you tonight, although I suspect shock would better describe Nadia's reaction. I really like you in this,' he added touching the filmy fabric of her dress.

'Armour,' Vanessa told him dryly, 'and when I saw the three of you sitting there I needed it. What was going on?'

'Jay wanted to talk to us both about Nadia's photographs—the ones we did to replace the ones of you. He doesn't want to admit it, but Nadia's aren't as good. She's still a first rate model and knows her stuff, but she lacks a certain something that came through on the ones we took of you. A sort of wholesomeness,' Gavin told her, grinning a little when he saw her expression.

'You make me sound like a breakfast cereal,' she grumbled, 'and personally I can't see Jay preferring my wholesome image to Nadia's exotic one.'

'Perhaps not personally, but there's no doubt in my opinion which ones come across best for the publicity shots. The thing is the whole idea was to use Nadia's name, so naturally we can't use your shots, and although Jay doesn't want to admit yours were better, he does feel, as I do, that Nadia just isn't coming across as we'd hoped. But what about you? I thought you'd sworn off all men?'

'Not all,' Vanessa corrected him coolly, 'just one. I'm not going to give Jay the satisfaction of knowing how much he hurt me Gavin. Besides I like Jeff, he's good fun.'

'Umm, well if you're going to start playing games, just remember that there's safety in numbers, won't you?' Oh, and before I forget,' he turned, one hand on the kitchen door handle, 'Jay told me to tell you he wants you to report to the club tomorrow. Pre-season training starts then and he wants you there to record it.'

Her brother's mention of her new assignment reminded Vanessa of her own idea. Briefly she outlined it to Gavin, waiting for his opinion.

'I like the sound of it, and of course,' he added, giving her an oblique smile, 'Jeff Marsden would make an excellent subject. He's been playing football for well over ten years and for some of the top clubs. Do you want to broach the subject with Jay or shall I?'

'Let me do some preliminary work on it, and then I'll talk to him about it. It might help if I actually have something to show him before I tackle him with it.'

'See how it goes,' Gavin counselled. 'There's nothing to stop you from taking the sort of photographs you'll need, in addition to doing the routine stuff. If you still want to go ahead in a month or so's time, then you can approach Jay.' He frowned as he opened the door. 'You know, I got the distinct impression that Nadia's got something on her mind, and I wouldn't be surprised if it wasn't becoming Mrs Jay Courtland.' He saw Vanessa's face and muttered a curse under his breath. 'I'm sorry Van, but you know dear Nadia, what Nadia wants . . .'

'Nadia goes right out and gets, yes I know. I'm going to bed Gavin. I'm tired, and if I'm going to start work in the morning . . .'

She was shaking when she reached the sanctuary of her room, cursing herself for being so weak. She had half suspected it anyway, surely? After all Jay had all the attributes Nadia looked for in her men; wealth, position, potent sexuality, and she had always known that her cousin was looking for the kind of marriage that would provide her with financial security, Nadia had never made any secret of it. If Jay did marry her cousin and they made their home at the manor she would have to leave Clarewell. The coward's way out, she taunted herself as she prepared for bed; running away to escape her pain, but what virtue was there in staying and being confronted every day by the knowledge that the man she loved was married to her cousin; that he preferred Nadia's shallow greed to her own love?

She forced herself to concentrate on Jeff, to remember how much she had enjoyed his company, to think about her new assignment. Perhaps it might prove to be the key to unlock other doors for her; a job in London, or even abroad. Go on, she mocked herself as she slid into bed, keep right on singing in the dark, keep right on trying to pretend that ... That what? That she wasn't still torn and bleeding inside? That she still didn't ache for Jay until the pain was a dull agony that threatened to obliterate everything else?

'Umm, very workmanlike,' Gavin commented as he studied Vanessa's jeans and sweatshirt clad figure. 'I'll run you down to the club shall I, and then you can give me a ring when you're through, and I'll pick you up. I've got to do some more work on those shots with Nadia this afternoon, so I've got to go down there.'

Training had just begun when Vanessa walked on to the team's practice ground. The cool breeze made her glad of the fleecy warmth of her sweatshirt as she watched the men obeying the instructions of the team coach, quickly setting up her equipment, professionalism taking over as she studied angles and switched lenses, waiting for the first signs of exhaustion to appear on the concentrating faces before she began to work. After half an hour her own muscles began to ache in sympathy with the footballers. Shirts clung damply to sweat streaked bodies, half a dozen or so breathless protests muttered when the coach insisted on repeats on some of the exercises.

'Okay you can take a break now,' Vanessa heard him call, 'but only for five minutes, we've a hell of a lot of hard work ahead of us.'

Three new players had been brought into the team, and Vanessa took some shots of them as the training formation broke up, noticing the way they hung together, separate from the other players. It would be interesting to watch their integration or lack of it with the rest of the team, over the coming months. There had been animosity in the team to the moves, and Vanessa wondered how they would adjust to it.

As she watched, Jeff detached himself from the main group of players and loped across, murmuring something to the newcomers and patting the youngest heartily on the back, saying something that brought a brief smile, before he turned and ran easily across the field to where Vanessa was standing.

'How can you,' she teased as he reached her, 'my muscles are already aching in protest.'

'Oh it's not so bad, I try to keep in training out of season. The older you get the harder it is to get back into the routine if you don't. A young player, like Harris for instance, can throw all the rules out of the window out of season, but when you get to my age,' he grimaced, bending to massage his calf. 'Like I said before this is going to be my last season. Financially I'm pretty well secure but . . .'

'But it's going to be a wrench giving it all up?' Vanessa supplied for him.

'In many ways, just as leaving the security of the known for the unknown always is a wrench. Most men are creatures of habit; that's why it's so hard for them to get married,' he added with a grin. 'Fear of the unknown!'

'Oh that's what it is, is it?' Vanessa laughed with

him, but there was a grain of truth in what he said, whether it was emotional or physical, most people did have a thread of fear of the unknown, of giving up what was safe and familiar for unchartered waters.

'Oh ho, here's the boss,' Vanessa heard Jeff mutter, 'I'd better go, he's not a bad guy,' he added, 'after all he's been through it all himself; he's gone from knowing the adulation that every top performer gets to being just another man in the street. I must say I'm delighted that you've been assigned as our official photographer,' Jeff told her as he prepared to leave her, 'especially when it comes to the away matches.'

'I thought a strict "no sex" rule was imposed during the run up to matches?' Vanessa said dryly.

Jeff smiled and winked at her. 'Sometimes there is,' he agreed, 'but you don't get to be an old hand like me without learning some of the dodges.'

They were both laughing when Jay reached them, his mouth tightening as he said curtly, 'Save it for off pitch if you don't mind Jeff. Are you finished here?' he asked Vanessa, his back towards Jeff, who pulled a wryly expressive face at Vanessa before going back to join the rest of the team, heading for the indoor gymnasium.

'I think I've got everything I need for now,' Vanessa responded coolly, 'but I'd like to get some shots in the gym.' She glanced at the heavy workmanlike watch she was wearing. 'Gavin isn't picking me up for a while yet, so there's plenty of time.'

'The Volvo's got a flat tyre,' Jay told her.

'Gavin just rang to tell me. He wants you to take over the session with Nadia.'

There was no way she was going to let him see just how much his pronouncement had affected her. 'Fine,' she said calmly, 'I'll just pack up this lot and I'll be there.'

She had left the bulk of her equipment in the club itself and she was glad of her familiarity with her task as her fingers worked automatically packing away lenses and stand, every movement economical and sure, never betraying her inner agitation or the weak pulse-racing turmoil inside her that Jay's proximity aroused. Of all the stupid, emotional females, she must surely take first prize she thought self mockingly. Jay didn't want her, he had made that more than plain, and yet here she was, a quivering responsive bundle of nerves and tissue, reduced to a state of helpless responsiveness; of virginal tremulousness, simply because he was standing next to her.

When she had finished packing away her equipment, he lifted the case before she could object, forcing her to trot helplessly behind him as he strode towards the club. He was wearing jeans and a checked shirt, the jeans moulding his thighs, making her intensely aware of the hard muscled length of his legs as she struggled to keep pace with him. She had seen this morning a little of the gruelling regime the team imposed on their bodies; Jay had once been like them and it showed in the taut musculature of his body. Unconsciously her glance drifted towards him, only to be hurriedly dragged away as she realised what she was doing.

As they stepped into the club building Jay

explained curtly that he wanted her to re-take the shots of Nadia with the team. 'No doubt Gavin has told you that we're not satisfied with the ones he's already done.'

'He did mention it,' Vanessa agreed quietly, following him into the changing room and setting up the equipment she would need. If he had planned it deliberately he could not have dreamed up anything more calculated to cause her anguish, she thought bitterly, but Jay could scarcely be held responsible for the Volvo's flat tyre. Apart from the obvious antipathy between herself and Nadia, the fact that Jay had made it plain that in his eyes she came nowhere near to equalling her cousin in sexuality or experience, there was also the added problem that she had never shot any semi-glamour scenes before. Still, Nadia was an experienced model as Gavin had said and surely far too professional to let her dislike of her cousin interfere with the photographs Vanessa was going to have to shoot.

The team was assembled in the pool when Nadia emerged from a changing cubicle, wearing only the very brief bottom of a bikini, her breasts taut and golden from the tan she maintained all the year round. At first she didn't see Vanessa who was busy with her equipment, but ran straight over to Jay, sliding her hands up inside the open neck of his shirt, her voice husky and low as she murmured, 'Darling ... you *are* here ... How lovely! You can take me out for lunch and then we can go back to your place. I should have stayed last night, but after you'd shown me round the manor ... It's going to be fantastic when it's finished. How much longer? A month or so, did you say?'

Her body was coiled sinuously against Jay's, but after registering it with sick clarity Vanessa was too busy trying to prise her heart free from the giant fist that enclosed it, squeezing the life blood out of it, to look again at the entwined couple. Nadia's voice was low enough only to reach her, and her whole body shook with the knowledge that she had been right; Jay had been at the manor with Nadia last night. Out of the corner of her eye she saw Nadia disentangle herself and stroll towards the pool. 'This time, Gavin darling, try not to make a botch of it,' she called over her shoulder, halting when Vanessa made no response to turn, her eyes dilating in furious dislike as she saw who was standing by the camera.

'Jay! What's she doing here?' she demanded angrily, 'God, it's bad enough having to endure Gavin's amateur attempts at professionalism—I've only put up with them for your sake, but I *won't* put up with this. Get her out of here and get me a proper photographer, someone who knows what he's doing.'

'I've already agreed that Gavin is to retain the contract,' Jay told her calmly. 'And as he's broken down, and Vanessa was here . . .'

'I am not having her taking my photograph.' Storm signals began to gather in the sapphire blue eyes, a sign that Vanessa knew of old. Nadia in a temper tantrum had to be seen to be believed; spoiled almost from the moment of her birth, the moment anything had not gone her way she had indulged in what often amounted to a bout of hysterics. And now, unless Vanessa was mistaken, Jay was about to be subjected to one. Vanessa saw him frown as though unable to equate the suave, sophisticated model with the woman now standing in front of him.

'You agreed we had to re-shoot the scene,' he reminded Nadia calmly, 'we went over it last night . . .'

'With Gavin,' Nadia interrupted him, 'with Gavin darling.' Her temper had subsided and she walked across to Jay, placing long scarlet finger nails on his arm, softly caressing it through the fabric of his shirt, anger replaced by an openly sensual smile as she continued to stroke his skin. 'Please try to understand . . . I just don't feel happy about being photographed by a woman— any woman, and besides,' her eyes darted malignant flames of hatred at Vanessa, 'bearing in mind Vanessa's jealousy of me, I just don't feel happy about her taking the shots. You do understand, don't you darling?' Her eyelashes fluttered, mouth pouting. 'Don't be cross,' she begged huskily, 'I promise I'll make it up to you . . . later.'

Feeling acutely sick, Vanessa didn't wait to hear Jay's response, simply packing up the equipment she had just assembled, her back towards her cousin and Jay. It wasn't simply that she was jealous that Jay should prefer Nadia, she felt sick with disappointment that the man she loved could prefer the type of shallow relationship that Nadia indulged in to the commitment she had wanted to give him.

There had been so many brief, casual relationships in his life that he obviously preferred them. 'I'm glad we both know the score,' he had said to her when he thought she was Nadia. A sudden rush of tears almost blinded her as she bent to pick up her case.

'Here, let me.' Jeff materialised at her side. 'Where's your car?'

'I haven't got one. Gavin was going to collect me. I'll call a taxi.'

'No, I'll take you home,' he brushed aside her protests picking up her case. Her altercation with Nadia had left her feeling so weak and shaky that Vanessa was glad to accept his support; his solid and reliable masculinity protecting her from having to look at Jay or her cousin.

'Well, how are you feeling about your first "away" game?'

They were four weeks into the season, and Vanessa was now on first name terms with most of the players, quite happy to sit in the coach with them as it took them down the motorway to their first away game.

'Apprehensive, but excited,' she admitted. Never a sport buff she was amazed at how involved she had become with the team, owning to herself that she had been guilty of mental discrimination against sportsmen in the past, thinking that their sport comprised their whole lives whereas, in fact, she had discovered that the majority of them had other widespread interests, ranging from literature and music to chess and art.

'Umm, well what I'm looking forward to is the bash Jay's giving at the manor later this year,' the

young goalkeeper Steve Richards, commented
with a grin. 'I hear the work is almost finished
now. You live close by, how's it looking?'

'I really don't know.' She wasn't going to admit
that Jay had not invited her to visit the manor to
take photographs of the work as it progressed, as
he had once suggested. That assignment had fallen
to Gavin, who was extremely enthusiastic about all
the alterations and improvements Jay was having
carried out. One of the second floor rooms had
been converted into a billiard room, and downstairs
the conservatory had been rebuilt complete with
an indoor swimming pool and a luxurious growth
of greenery.

'I'd settle down and try to snatch some sleep if I
were you,' Jeff suggested at her elbow. They were
sitting together, and although he smiled at her
Vanessa could see the lines of strain round his eyes
and mouth. Although Jeff himself hadn't discussed
it with her she had heard the other players talking
about his game, and she had seen for herself the
slight slowing down of his reflexes which could be
critical to the team's performance on the pitch. He
still had the experience and skill which had carried
him to the top of his profession, but time was
running out for him. Vanessa sensed how
important it was for him to do well in what she
knew would be his last season as a professional
player, but she also knew that a certain amount of
antipathy existed between him and Jay, which was
surprising when she reflected that Jay too had
experienced what Jeff was going through now.

Jay! She was beginning to think he was like
Rome. All thoughts seemed to lead indirectly to

him. He and Nadia were now almost a recognised couple, and Vanessa lived in dread of hearing them announce their engagement, perhaps they would at the ball Jay was holding. Or perhaps they would simply slip away and get married, although somehow she couldn't imagine Nadia relinquishing the publicity and furore of a lavish engagement party and an even more lavish and undoubtedly expensive ring. She would have given anything not to attend the ball, but common sense told her that there was no way she could get out of it; at least not without betraying to Jay that she was still foolishly and humiliatingly besotted with him.

The match the team were playing in was just outside London. In order to make sure the team had sufficient rest, there was an overnight stop on Friday with the match on the Saturday afternoon. Vanessa had the Saturday morning free and she intended to use it to find a suitable dress for the ball.

'Wake up, we're nearly there,' Jeff told her, his hand on her arm, his head bent towards her. As she smiled up at him Vanessa experienced a distinctly prickly sensation at the back of her neck and glanced round. Jay was sitting several seats behind on the opposite side of the aisle, the empty seat next to him spread with papers. He was looking straight at her, his eyes cold with dislike, flat and yellow. She shivered, remembering the warning he had given her only the other day. He did not want Jeff becoming involved with her emotionally, he had told her, it might affect the player's game.

'If he wants to keep his place on the team, it will

mean total concentration,' Jay had said curtly. 'He's in a very vulnerable position at the moment, and if he's got any sense he won't jeopardise it by taking on an emotional commitment he doesn't have the time to handle.'

'Don't you think he's old enough to make his own decisions on that?' she had retaliated, angry spots of colour springing to life on her otherwise pale skin. She had had the feeling he would have gone on to say something else if Nadia hadn't interrupted them. Nadia! Her cousin had disdained to watch tomorrow's match, opting instead to spend the weekend with some old friends.

The team was occupying almost an entire floor of the hotel they were staying at, and although the long drive had left Vanessa too tired to join the others in the restaurant for a meal, as soon as she had unpacked and inspected the luxury of a room with its own bar, TV, superbly equipped bathroom, and a small balcony overlooking the gardens, Vanessa ordered herself a snack from room service, and promised herself an early night.

Jeff had offered to buy her dinner, but Vanessa had compromised by suggesting that he take her out after the match instead.

'To celebrate or commiserate?' he had responded lightly. 'Okay, you've got a date.'

Their relationship hadn't progressed any further than the pleasantly friendly footing on which it had started, and that was what Vanessa preferred. She had told Jeff quite frankly that there could be nothing more, and he had accepted her decision without questioning it too deeply for which she was grateful.

She was awake early on the Saturday morning and breakfasted in her room, determined to pack as much shopping into her morning as she could. At the reception desk she learned that it would take her just over half an hour to travel into the city, and she left without seeing Jeff who she knew would be training with the rest of the team during the morning.

She found the dress she wanted with astonishing ease, in a small boutique off South Molton Street. It was the sort of dress that dreams are made of; very 'Gone with the Wind' with a full, rustling skirt, in a soft pink silk taffeta. Vanessa knew even before she tried it on that she was going to buy it. The tight fitting bodice made her waist look tiny, the skirt rustling provocatively when she walked. She would wear her hair up, she decided, studying her reflection in the mirror, and buy some satin shoes to match the dress. The expertly cut neckline gave a tantalising glimpse of her cleavage when she moved, and she wrote out a cheque for what was really a frighteningly astronomical sum with so little guilt that she surprised herself.

She was back at the hotel in time for lunch. Jeff was keyed up and tense and so they didn't talk much, Vanessa quickly changing to her working clothes of jeans and sweat shirt as she gathered up her camera and equipment, dashing back downstairs to take photographs of the players as the pre-match tension began to make itself felt.

She went with them to the ground, and sat with the team coach during the match.

It was a narrow victory for the team, with them winning two-one. There had been a chance for an extra goal and Vanessa's heart had been in her mouth as she watched Jeff take it, but somehow his shot had been mistimed and missed the goal mouth by centimetres. He was frowning and withdrawn when they eventually came off the pitch.

Anxious to fulfil her assignment properly Vanessa followed them back to the changing rooms, working quickly to capture the euphoria and end of match atmosphere pervading the small, utilitarian room, leaving only when high spirits threatened her with a ducking from the younger members of the team.

Back at the hotel she showered and changed for dinner and then sat down to wait for Jeff. When eight thirty came and went and he had still not appeared she telephoned his room. When there was no response she put down the receiver, frowning thoughtfully. If Jeff had wanted to break their date there was no reason why he should not do so—there was no emotional commitment or tie between them beyond that of friends, and he had always struck her as far too polite to simply let her down without any explanation or apology. So where was he? Anxiety crept into her eyes as she remembered how withdrawn he had been after the match, and how Jay had drawn him to one side. It was Jeff's constant fear that he would lose his place in the team before the end of the season, although he tried to appear lighthearted about the possibility.

Coming to a quick decision Vanessa left her own room and hurried down the corridor to Jeff's. She knocked briefly on the door and when there was no response tried the handle. It opened inwards and she went inside, not totally surprised to see Jeff sprawled on the bed, his eyes closed.

'Jeff?' She shook his shoulder, and his eyes opened.

'Vanessa?' he glanced at his watch and swore. 'God I'm sorry. Our date!' he shook his head. 'I was so wound up when I got back here that I had a few drinks.' He gestured to the bottle and glass on the table. 'I must have fallen asleep. You saw what happened this afternoon?'

Sensing that he wanted to talk Vanessa sat down in the chair by the bed. 'It could have happened to anyone,' she said reasonably.

'But it happened to me. I've had a brief talk with Jay about it. He's going to give me another chance, but if I muff another shot like that one, I'm going to be off the team, I'm sure of it. Oh he didn't come right out and say so, but the hint was there plain enough.' He pushed his hand tiredly through his hair. 'Look I'm not going to be much company tonight, how about taking a rain-check on dinner?'

'How about eating here?' Vanessa suggested lightly, not wanting to leave him alone to brood. 'They're showing quite a good film tonight, we could watch that.'

Jeff's face softened as he looked at her. 'You know you're quite a woman Vanessa March. The kind that sticks with a man through good and bad; the kind a man would be a fool not to hold on to if he got the chance. And the kind who only wants me as a friend because she's in love with someone else,' he added huskily. 'Am I right?'

'Jeff . . .'

'Look it's okay,' he held up his hands. 'I know when I'm trespassing. Let's get that dinner ordered shall we. Suddenly I have an almighty appetite.'

It was just after eleven o'clock when Vanessa let herself out of Jeff's room. They had spent a pleasant evening together, talking and watching television; or at least Jeff had talked and she had listened. Wrapped up in her own thoughts she bumped into someone walking down the corridor, strong fingers clamping on to her shoulders, cold yellow eyes flicking from her face to the door she had just closed behind her.

'Well, well,' Jay taunted softly. 'Still trying to get rid of your virginity? What's the matter, won't Jeff take it either?'

Her hand streaked upwards automatically, the sharp sound of her open palm connecting with his cheek preternaturally loud in the silence of the hotel corridor.

Jay reacted swiftly, lean fingers clamping down over her hand, imprisoning it against his skin so that she could feel the blood beating up underneath it, and a rush of dizzying reaction raced through her.

'It's called sexual frustration,' he mocked grimly, watching the colour flare up under her skin, 'and since I'm suffering from it as well, we might as well relieve it together . . . That's something you're going to have to learn if you stay around football players for very long. When they're down they want mothering, not . . .' He bit out a harsh exclamation as her imprisoned fingers curled raking across his skin in a furious reaction to his open contempt.

Vanessa withdrew from him immediately, fleeing instinctively for the sanctuary of her room. She barely recognised him in this aggressively sexual mood, but her flight seemed only to intensify rather than douse his predatory instincts. He caught her as she reached the door, pushing her inside and then closing it behind them and pocketing the key.

'Jay, I don't know what you think you're doing...' she began breathlessly, backing away from him, but he cut her short, with a softly grating laugh.

'You may not, but I do,' he told her watching her as he came towards her. A man likes to celebrate his triumphs, and the best place I know for celebrating is in bed...'

'Surely the last place you'd want me,' Vanessa reminded him coldly, trying to hang on to the rags of reason she still possessed. 'Dross? Wasn't that how you described me? The woman you want tonight is Nadia, Jay.'

'But she isn't here,' he retaliated softly, 'and you are. *Did* he take it?' he probed further.

'Take what?' Vanessa felt as though she was fast losing control of the situation.

'That precious virginity you were going to barter for a wedding ring. Because if he hasn't, tonight I will. That's what you want isn't it Vanessa? To lie in my arms, my body possessing yours?'

CHAPTER EIGHT

'No!' Her denial lay heavily in the air between them, but it had taken her several seconds to summon it, several seconds during which she was sure that Jay had recognised the hunger warring with the course every instinct urged upon her. He didn't want *her*; all he wanted was a facsimile of Nadia. If she let him so much as touch her while he felt like this, she would be destroying her own self respect for ever. Hastily she backed away from him, recognising the tiny flames licking hungrily in his eyes.

'No? I think you mean yes,' he told her thickly. 'In fact I'm going to prove to you that you *do* mean yes.'

What on earth had got into him? That his actions were even partially motivated by what he had described as 'frustration' seemed difficult to believe when he had only been apart from Nadia for a mere night.

A phrase she had once heard her cousin use gloatingly in connection with another of her lovers came back to her, 'He's hardly a once a day man sweetie,' Nadia had commented watching the colour flood her face. That description could apply equally well to Jay, but in his case Vanessa had always believed that he was the one who controlled his sexual desires rather than the other way around.

There was nothing remotely controlled about his expression now. Eyes the colour of rich topaz glittered between thick black lashes, his hooded aroused scrutiny of her sending shivers of response through her body, tormenting every nerve ending. The dark hair was ruffled, his white shirt unfastened at the throat, his skin warmly olive and enticingly masculine. But it wasn't *her* he wanted, Vanessa reminded herself fiercely; that desire barely held in check; that hot, barely restrained need was not for *her*, but for her cousin.

'You want me Vanessa.' He said it thickly as though surprised to find the words on his tongue. 'No matter what you've shared with Marsden you're still aching to know what it would be like with me. Aren't you. *Aren't you?*'

He had reached her, imprisoning her with the hands that bit into her waist, almost shaking the response he wanted out of her. 'You can't hide it from me Vanessa. Your body's shaking with it; with wanting me.' She heard the slurred, masculine satisfaction in his voice and wondered wildly if he'd been drinking and if this was the reason for his totally unexpected behaviour.

'If I'm shaking it's because, you're shaking me so hard,' Vanessa managed valiantly. 'Please let me go Jay. And please leave my room. I don't know why you came in here, I . . .'

'I came in here because I want to make love to you,' she heard Jay replying rawly. 'Because I *am* going to make love to you.'

He was beyond reason Vanessa thought wildly, beyond anything, deaf to everything but the voice of his own desire. 'Jay I'm not Nadia,' she reminded him, trying to evade the lean fingers gripping her soft flesh. In the morning she would be bruised. And not only physically an inner voice warned her. She must get him out of her room, for the sake of her sanity and her self respect.

'No, you're not,' he agreed, 'but you look like her.' He bent towards her and unbelievably Vanessa smelled the spirits on his breath. He *had* been drinking. To celebrate the team's victory? Surely not to the extent that would cause him to behave like this?

It was as though every restraint and caution had been removed; as though she was seeing him for the first time, and what she saw both frightened and aroused her. And therein lay her own danger. She wanted badly to succumb to him, to actively encourage him to touch her, to make love to her, but she could not. His fingers found the buttons of her shirt and he had half of them unfastened before she could stop him, the angry barrier of her fingers contemptuously brushed aside, her wrists captured in a bone-bruising grip, his free hand flicking aside the protection of her blouse to reveal the firm swell of her breasts in their brief covering of lace. Her body seemed to possess a will of its own, her nipples thrusting eagerly against the confining fabric, a shudder of fiercely dark pleasure surging through her as Jay bent his head and drew his tongue delicately along the valley between her breasts, his fingers deftly finding the front fastening and freeing her soft curves from their unwanted imprisonment.

'Jay, please don't do this.' Her voice was a tortured whisper in her throat, reason and sanity abandoning her as his hand slipped inside her blouse to cup the satiny flesh of one breast, his tongue spiralling delicately against her skin a mere breath away from the pink nipple, flaunting her arousal with shameless abandonment.

She had to do something and quickly before she was completely lost. Summoning all her strength of will she forced herself away from him grasping the gaping sides of her blouse and pulling them defensively against her body, unaware of how her action drew attention to the full curves of her breasts. 'Jay, I'm *not* Nadia,' she said huskily, 'and I won't stand in for her, even if I was physically capable of doing so. I'm afraid my expertise falls very far short of hers,' she added with unconscious bitterness.

'Your *expertise* might,' Jay agreed laconically, showing no signs of accepting her dismissal, 'but your enthusiasm more than makes up for it, and as I remember you were very enthusiastic the last time I held you in my arms, weren't you, Vanessa?'

Cruel of him to remind her of that now, to re-ignite the ache that tormented her body, overruling the voice that warned her that she was acutely vulnerable to this man and that it would be wiser to hold him at a distance. Wiser perhaps, but when was a woman in love ever wise? Vanessa shuddered and as though he recognised it as a gesture of defeat Jay moved indolently towards her, his fingers curling into the fabric of her blouse just above her own. Her need to cover her nudity from him was lost beneath a more urgent need to escape. Arms extended stiffly in front of her she tried to fend him off, but he merely smiled supinely, a flash of white teeth in the darkness of her lamplit room. Her hands made contact with the powerful thrust of his chest, fingers scrabbling unsteadily against his skin as defeat loomed up over her. Lean hands curled tighter into the fabric of her blouse wrenching it apart with a savage movement to expose her breasts, brown knuckles gleaming against the mother of pearl skin as he stared down at her and then slowly bent his head.

'No!' The protest was torn from her throat. She could feel her heart pounding with fear, feel the tension getting ready to explode inside her, and yet when the caress she had dreaded never came it was disappointment that sent her stomach plunging downwards and not relief.

'This has gone far enough, Jay,' she whispered faintly. 'Please leave now.'

'Or you'll do what? Cry rape?' He shook his head. 'No, I'm not leaving, Vanessa. Not until you tell me exactly what the relationship is between you and Marsden.'

Anger flared hot and searing deep inside her. How dare he invade her privacy, question her private life; walk into her room and make love to her simply because he was drunk and she looked like the woman who shared his bed; the woman he had *chosen* to share his bed. She reminded herself.

'What's the matter,' she demanded bitterly, 'having second thoughts, Jay?' she taunted him. 'Thinking that if you had played your cards right you could have had Nadia's experience and my . . . virginity?'

She heard him swear, but the anger consuming her was too powerfully in control to be dammed now. She felt violently, wonderfully free of all constraints; free to say and do exactly what she pleased.

'Have you slept with him? Have you?' He was shaking her again making her head spin, her senses dazed by the musky aroused scent of his body and the whisky fumes breathed into her skin.

'What could it possibly matter to you? You've already said that you don't want me, unless it's as a substitute for Nadia. Well Jeff wants me for myself . . .'

'He wants you as a shoulder to cry on, damn you,' she heard Jay curse as she was hauled against his body, 'and if you aren't going to tell me if you gave yourself to him there's only one way for me to find out, isn't there?'

Something was very wrong. She ought to have been feeling dismay and apprehension, and certainly she ought to have been cautioning restraint, urging Jay to think again, reminding him that he had been drinking; that he preferred Nadia, but instead what she did feel was a gloriously heady sense of power; an inner knowledge that he had left behind the self-control he normally exercised, and that the male body, moulded so close to her own was fully and unashamedly aroused.

'Jay.' She made a token protest which was summarily ignored, his hands dealing swiftly with the zip of her skirt, and then lifting her free of the dark puddle of clothes at her feet as he carried her over to the bed. She shuddered deeply as his mouth nuzzled against her throat, capturing the pulse that thudded there, his mouth opening over

her own with a raw heat that blasted away
common sense and invoked a blind response to the
hungry invasion of his tongue. There was no
subtlety in Jay's kiss, only an intense raw need that
pulverised her defences, eliciting a response that
burned along her nerve endings, her body arching
mutely beneath the heated stroke of his hands.

Her mouth was released, her lips faintly swollen,
the taste of his lingering still on her tongue.
Somehow her hands had found their way inside his
shirt and were caressing the hard bones of his
shoulders. 'Take it off.' The hoarse command was
muttered against the soft skin of her throat
causing her to swallow in mute response to the
rough sensuality of his demand, the faint betraying
movement subjected to the caress of his tongue
and lips. 'Take it off,' Jay repeated with quiet
savagery, 'and then kiss me the way you did him.'

It was as though she possessed no will of her
own. Her fingers found the small buttons and
unfastened them, her hands returning to his
shoulders, gliding lightly over the hard bones,
pushing aside his shirt, sliding it down his arms,
her breasts brushing against the warm flesh of his
chest. Her breath lodged somewhere in her throat
as he touched her breasts caressing their swollen
contours, drawing tantalising circles round her
nipple with the tip of his tongue. She released her
breath rawly, whispering his name as an aching
protest, but it was too late. Her body ached
fiercely for his possession, and his eyes held the
blind aroused glitter of a man too caught up in the
intensity of his own desire to listen. Her hands
fanned across his chest, her nails accidentally

scraping across his flat nipples. The accidental
contact acted as a catalyst causing a shudder to
wrench through him, the hoarse cry of pleasure he
muttered lost as his mouth found her breast.

Fierce darts of pleasure knifed through her,
followed by a weak langour that left her boneless
as a small cat, her spine arching as she sought
unconsciously to prolong the contact.

'You're driving me crazy, you know that don't
you?' Jay demanded feverishly, his mouth still
exploring her skin. 'Vanessa!' Her name was a
thick protest half lost as he turned into her body,
shuddering beneath the provocative rake of her
nails across the taut flatness of his belly. The
caress had been an automatic response to the
torment of his mouth against her breast and his
response electrified her with its intensity. Until
then she hadn't even realised that he had partially
discarded his pants, and he sat up quickly pulling
them off and throwing them on to the floor,
turning to lean his head against her stomach, the
heavy, dark weight of it pillowed against her,
turning her insides to melting surrender, her
fingers caressing the shape of his skull through the
thick darkness of his hair.

One hand cradled her hip, his tongue exploring
the soft indentation of her navel, and then beyond
to the lacy line of her briefs, his hand releasing her
hip to stroke up over her thigh, sliding beneath the
silky fabric. Vanessa felt herself tense, and knew
he felt her tension as his fingers released the fabric
and instead cupped the soft flesh of her bottom. It
was ridiculous to feel shy and self-conscious, but
for some reason she did. The moonlight through

the uncurtained window gilded Jay's nakedness with silver. He was watching her through the darkness and acting on some impulse she barely understood, she ran her fingers lightly down the silver outline, tracing the indentation of his waist and the hard thrust of his hip. Her fingers reached the top of his thigh when he stopped them trapping them against his skin with his free hand.

His head was still pillowed against her body, his teeth gently nibbling the tender flesh of her waist as he murmured. 'If you want to go any further, first you'll have to pay a forfeit.'

When she didn't move he laughed softly, stroking her skin with his tongue. 'Perhaps I'll make you pay it anyway. Did Marsden kiss you like this?' he asked her trailing light kisses down past her hip, down to the lacy barrier of her briefs. Her stomach was in turmoil, her nerves loud in their protest, the clamour of their fear fighting with the sexual excitement building up inside her.

'Well?' He followed the line of her briefs to where it was no more than a tiny lace-covered strip of elastic, stroking his tongue along her skin. Her fingers trembled against his thigh and then drew away as though his skin stung.

'Jay . . .'

'Too late,' he told her thickly. 'You'll have to pay the forfeit now.' His mouth was teasing her skin, burning it with brief kisses, his hand leaving her bottom to caress her inner thigh. It was becoming impossible almost to breathe, never mind to think. The brief barrier she had wanted to retain in a sudden access of shy modesty had become an unbearable and subtle instrument of torture that Jay was using against her, and she cried out a muffled protest as his tongue traced the scalloped indentations of lace, his thumb tracing lazy, spiralling circles of pleasure against the silky inner flesh of her thigh that was a torment in itself.

'You still want me Vanessa.' It was said with an assurance that she knew she would remember later with humiliation, but right now nothing was more important than the union her body was craving for. 'They say a woman never forgets her first lover, but tonight I can make you forget Marsden, can't I?'

'Jay?' she moved against him in a gesture both convulsive and pleading, her body trembling when she saw the glitter of passion turning his eyes molten gold.

'Touch me, Vanessa,' he muttered thickly, closing his eyes. 'Can't you tell how much I want that? Nadia wouldn't need to be asked.'

It was like a knife in her heart. She glanced down to where his hand lay over the whiteness of her briefs and shuddered with acute self-disgust, willing her body not to respond to the intoxication of his touch.

'I'm not Nadia, Jay.' How flat and empty her voice sounded, all pleasure and warmth gone from it as it was gone from her body. 'Nor as desperate as you seem to think.' She said it quietly, but knew from the sudden tension of his body where it touched hers, that he understood.

'Meaning that Marsden hasn't made love to you?' he queried softly. 'Meaning that you're still hoping I'm going to be the one to . . .' He moved away from her so abruptly that her body shivered in shocked recognition of his rejection.

'You were the one who forced his way in here Jay . . .'

'I'd been drinking,' he told her sardonically. 'Surely you realised that?'

The harsh mockery of his words rang in her ears long after he had left her. Twice now she had let Jay Courtland hurt and humiliate her almost beyond bearing. There wasn't going to be a third time, she told herself savagely. And this time she had no one to blame but herself. What had happened to her pride, her self respect? Was she so dementedly in love, so hungry for his touch, his possession that she wanted them at any price?

No! She said the word fiercely, marching into her bathroom and turning on the shower. Half an hour later, her recalcitrant body suitably chastised, her skin glowing from the sting of the cold water she had subjected it to, she crawled into the bed she had so recently lain on with Jay, her body entwined with his. Never again was he going to get another opportunity to humiliate her she vowed as she tried to court sleep, firmly banishing from her mind tormenting visions of Jay lying beside her, his body taut and sleek, beautifully proportioned, arousingly male. With a small groan she rolled over on to her stomach squeezing her eyes closed willing the unwanted image away.

After breakfast the following morning when she got on the coach that was to take them back to Clarewell there was no sign of Jay.

'Looks like the boss must have gone to collect his woman,' Vanessa heard one of the players comment. Sickness hit her in the pit of her stomach; the old familiar hatred of taking second place to Nadia, of being used as her cousin's substitute. She was glad of Jeff's deep concentration on the book he was reading during the journey back because it freed her from the need to make conversation. Like her he looked pale and tense, but at least there was a possibility that Jeff would be able to resolve his problems while hers threatened to follow her for the rest of her life.

CHAPTER NINE

'VAN, these are really good,' Gavin enthused holding several prints up to the light. 'You've really managed to capture the mood of the players.' As he put down the prints he gave them another admiring look. 'The post match euphoria and pre-match tension can almost be felt in these shots, Jay is going to be really pleased.'

Her brother never handed out flattery where his work was concerned, and Vanessa knew herself that the latest batch of photographs she had taken were good, and Gavin was right, the emotion of the players was almost a palpable feeling. She studied them again herself, knowing that she had every right to feel proud of her work. 'I shouldn't be surprised if you didn't end up with an award for this lot,' Gavin told her. 'They're more than simple publicity shots. This one of Marsden is particularly good.' He held up a photograph she had taken of Jeff as he left the pitch shoulders bowed in defeat, weary depression etched into every line of his face, dejection clinging to him like a second skin.

'Have you approached Jay yet with your idea for the new project?' Gavin asked, still studying her work. 'I think once he sees these he'll be very amenable.'

'I haven't seen him since we came back on Sunday.' It was now Friday, and Vanessa had learned at the club only that morning that Jay planned to attend the Saturday match with Nadia as his guest. The gossip columns were still full of photographs of them as a couple; whenever Vanessa saw Jay at the Club he always seemed to have Nadia with him. In another man she might have thought he was deliberately flaunting his conquest of her cousin, but Jay Courtland wasn't a man who needed to flaunt any woman to add to his consequence; he was a man complete unto himself. So why did she get the impression he was deliberately drawing attention to his relationship with Nadia? She had seen them in the car park together only yesterday, just emerging from Jay's Ferrari. She could have sworn he had seen her heading for the Volvo parked only yards away, but that hadn't stopped him taking Nadia in his arms, one hand resting possessively just below her breast as he kissed her. It had made her feel ill to see her cousin's lissom frame plastered along the lean length of Jay's body, her arms wrapped round his neck, her face lifting for his kiss. So, she was jealous! She tried to shrug her feelings aside; to tell herself that her love for Jay was something she simply had to suffer, like a bad bout of measles and that once it was over she would be cured for good. The trouble was she couldn't believe that it ever would be over. Each day increased the intensity of her pain and with it her longing for Jay's love. She was being a fool she warned herself over and over again; Jay had no earthly use for her unless it was as a substitute for her cousin on those few occasions when Nadia couldn't be with him. He had shown her over and over again that all he felt for her was contempt; he had held her up to ridicule; had humiliated and hurt her and yet she still dreamed at night that she was in his arms, and that the name he whispered against her skin was her own.

She wasn't sure what reaction he expected to get from her, but she did know that he watched her, coldly and challengingly, flat yellow eyes skimming her too pale and finely drawn features whenever he walked into the club and saw her there, and surely it wasn't simply her imagination that told her he caressed and touched Nadia more whenever he saw that she was there.

Oh yes, she knew exactly what he was doing. She wasn't that dense. He was underlining his preference for her cousin, telling her without words that *she* meant nothing to him; that it was the Nadias of this world he preferred and not the Vanessas. She had the feeling that he was waiting for something to happen but she didn't know that. What did he expect? That she would break down; cry; scream. It became a matter of pride with her never to betray any reaction at all to his presence or that of Nadia, who lost no opportunity of belittling her cousin. Vanessa shrugged it all aside, proud of the fact that no one, not even Gavin, guessed just how much effort it took. She had finally joined the adult world she acknowledged; had finally learned to play the game by the rules; and her own rules of play dictated that she never, ever betrayed to Jay again just how much he could and had hurt her.

The weeks slipped by and Vanessa established a pleasant routine. The more time she spent with the players, the more their differing personalities showed in the photographs she took. It became her recognisable trade-mark and one that sports fans looked for. Several of the pictures she took had received national coverage, and she had been approached by other football teams to do some publicity work for them. She had turned it down, as she had to do under the terms of Gavin's contract with Jay, concentrating instead on building up the portfolio she hoped to use on her profile of football players.

As the season progressed she was pleased to see that Jeff was holding his own, although she could see that the strain of doing this was telling on him. 'All I want to do is finish the season in style and then I'll call it quits,' he confessed to her. 'It wasn't so bad last year, the team wasn't doing as well as it is now, and there wasn't the new blood we have now to keep pace with, so I managed okay. This season I'm struggling. I know it, the rest of the team knows it, and Jay knows it.'

'But the younger players respect your experience Jeff.'

'Umm, maybe, all I know is that I won't be sorry to leave. Courtland is a hard taskmaster. He can afford the best and that's what he wants. Everyone laughed when they heard that he intended to take over a fourth division team and take it to the top, but no one's laughing now. You realise that if we keep on as we are, we'll be in with a chance for promotion to the third division next season?'

Vanessa did, and she sighed her acknowledgement, she had felt resentful of Jay when she first heard he was coming, but she had to admit that he had been as good as his word. The new sports complex was due to open shortly; the work on the manor was finished and the Christmas Ball only days away.

Clarewell as a town had an awful lot of reasons to be grateful to Jay Courtland. She herself had found out quite by chance of the large donation he had made to the local children's home. There were always free tickets for a party of children from the home to attend the team's matches, and Vanessa suspected that the new swimming pool being installed at the home was being paid for by Jay.

Vanessa had gone with Jay and Nadia to take photographs the day the new sports complex was officially handed over to the Town Council. 'And what do you think Vanessa?' Jay had asked her mockingly in an aside when he had received the grateful thanks of the Mayor.

'I think you've been very generous,' she had said quietly, not wanting to add more, not wanting to say that she could well understand why a boy who had had nothing should want to give so much to other potentially deprived children, but Nadia had caught her reply and interrupted.

'Of course he's been generous darling, and I shouldn't wonder if others are equally generous in their turn. Perhaps not this year or even next, but certainly the year after that...' When she saw Vanessa's expression she had laughed mockingly, 'Oh poor little innocent Vanessa doesn't know what I mean darling. I'm talking about the New Year Honours List, Vanessa, you know, rewards for good and brave deeds. You've planned it all so cleverly darling,' Nadia had cooed turning back to Jay, stroking the sleeve of his jacket in that intimate predatory way she had, her eyes openly assessing the future, 'starting with local good works, gradually building your way up.'

It isn't true, Vanessa had wanted to say, but the look in Jay's eyes had forestalled her, and she had turned blindly away, wanting only to escape before she could be hurt any more.

'I hope you've got something special to wear on Saturday,' Gavin commented. 'It's going to be a pretty swish do.'

'Yes, with half the county invited,' Vanessa agreed bitterly, 'so that Jay can do a little bit more canvassing for his knighthood.'

Gavin frowned. 'Oh come on, I know that's what Nadia believes, because it's just the sort of thing she would do, but surely you don't think Jay isn't genuine? After all, apart from the publicity angle for the football club he's taken a very low profile on the whole thing—deliberately so.'

Vanessa knew that Gavin spoke the truth, but the barb inflicted by Nadia still stung. There had been no doubt in Vanessa's mind that when Nadia perceived Jay with his knighthood, she pictured herself as his wife. Permanency had no place in his life Jay had told her; what he liked were women who knew the score. Obviously he had changed his mind, unless he had taken the cynical view that with Nadia he could have the best of both worlds. A wife to provide him with an heir; and a woman at the same time experienced enough to turn a blind eye to any liaisons her husband might choose to indulge in outside their marriage.

'Well, you still haven't told me?'

'Told you what?' Vanessa frowned, dragging her attention back to her brother.

'What you're going to wear for the ball?'

'Oh, I got something in London the first time I went down there to an away match.'

'You haven't seen the manor since all the work was finished have you? It's really fantastic. Jay's chosen all the furnishings himself. Said he wanted it to look like a home, not an ad in a glossy magazine. He even went to the lengths of digging back through the old records to see how it used to be furnished.'

Vanessa hadn't yet seen the manor for the very good reason that Jay had not invited her to. Gavin had been a constant visitor, and she had lost count of the times she had seen the white Ferrari roaring past the lodge, with Nadia in the passenger seat. She must be getting paranoid, she thought acidly; after all it was hardly feasible really that everything Jay did was deliberately designed to wound her, even though it seemed that way sometimes.

The day of the ball dawned sharp and clear; the sky a pale blue background for the tracery of bare winter branches. Delays in the completion of work on the manor had meant that the date of the ball had had to be put back until mid-December, and Vanessa shivered a little as she stepped out of the lodge, despite her cord jeans and thick jumper. For some reason she hadn't been able to sleep and rather than lie in bed she had got up intending to take a brisk walk. She had the morning to herself; a thin pale sun glinting on the frost that rimed the grass. Without conscious thought she found her feet taking her in the direction of the path that led through the copse that separated the lodge from the manor. A rabbit scudded furiously towards its burrow as she walked along the path, birds setting up a series of alarm calls, a thin sheet of ice mirrored the surface of the pool, the dry rasp of fallen leaves making a pleasant sound as she walked through them. Through the denuded trees she could see the house, and her heart gave a painful bound as she tried not to envisage Nadia there with Jay. That her cousin was to act as Jay's hostess was hardly surprising in the circumstances, what was stupid was that she should feel so much pain at the thought. She had known for months now what the situation was. She stumbled over an exposed tree root, biting back a startled exclamation as she fell, only to feel an even keener anxiety shooting through her as she heard the sound of horse's hoofs behind her. She got up shakily, more bruised than actually hurt, slowly turning in the direction the sounds were coming from. Jay was riding towards her mounted on a sleek black Arab. The horse pirouetted fiercely in front of her, its impatient movements easily controlled by the lean fingers grasping the reins.

'Well, well, trespassing again? You seem to be making a habit of this.'

The thick dark hair was ruffled by the breeze, close fitting jeans drawing her attention to powerful thigh muscles. Her breath seemed to have lodged somewhere in her throat and against her will Vanessa found her glance travelling along the length of his body over the thick cream sweater to the sardonic curling outline of his mouth, and the gold eyes that watched her with merciless scrutiny.

'I was simply taking a walk.'

'In private grounds,' Jay reminded her easing his weight slightly as the horse pranced impatiently on the path. 'And besides you weren't walking when I saw you, you were standing staring at the house. You've got a very vivid imagination or so Nadia tells me. She also told me that you used to pretend you owned this place when you were a child. Is that what you were doing just now Vanessa? Standing, imagining . . .'

'I must get back.' She interrupted him unsteadily unable to bear any more, skirting the prancing Arab, hoping that he would put her shaking down to cold and not the aching despair that seemed to have invaded every muscle. 'So must I,' Jay agreed. 'Nadia will be awake by now.' His eyes skimmed the outline of the house and Vanessa turned away, biting her lip to stop it from trembling. Why did he have to do this to her? Why was it so necessary for him to underline and reinforce his preference for her cousin?

'Yes, you mustn't keep her waiting,' she agreed coolly. 'I believe her time is . . . rather expensive.' It was a catty remark to make, and one she wished unsaid when she saw the hard glitter of anger darkening the gold eyes to topaz. 'While you of course give yours for free,' Jay said smoothly, 'Hasn't anyone ever told you yet Vanessa that a man values most what costs him dearest? If your cousin sets a high price on herself it's because she knows it's one I'm willing to pay.'

'That's because you're a cynic,' Vanessa threw

back at him, 'someone who thinks money can buy everything, someone . . .'

'Who knows the cost of everything and the value of nothing?' Jay drawled, 'is that what you're trying to say? What price would you put on your honesty, I wonder, Vanessa. I should be very interested to know.'

He wheeled the horse round and left her before she could respond, but even if she had been able to think of a fitting reply, she doubted that she would have been able to voice it. He had never forgiven her for pretending that she was Nadia; or was it himself he couldn't forgive because he had believed her, she wondered bitterly. Whichever one of them he blamed there was no doubt about who he intended to punish, extracting payment drop by drop, inflicting a series of small wounds that she sometimes felt would never heal. If she had any sense she would leave Clarewell now, but when did a woman in love ever exhibit good sense?

'How do I look?'

Vanessa twirled round slowly, watching the full skirts of her dress bell out gracefully. 'Gavin?' She turned her head to look worriedly at her brother when there was no response. He looked very attractive in his formal evening clothes, his fair hair slicked tidily off his forehead for once.

'Words fail me.' He said it slowly, shaking his head. 'Van, you look . . . beautiful.' He saw her face and said, 'I mean it. You've changed over these last months, lost weight here,' he touched the line of her cheek bone and jaw. 'You look as though the lightest breath would blow you away.'

'And the dress?'

'Worth every penny of the fortune I have no doubt it cost,' he assured her.

Vanessa glanced at her reflection checking that what her brother had said was true. The dark mass of her hair piled up on her head in soft curls drew attention to the slender length of her neck. At her ears she wore the pearl and diamond drop earrings that had been a twenty-first birthday present from Nadia's parents. She had lost weight as Gavin had said, giving her face an ethereal beauty emphasised by the deep sapphire of her eyes. Not wanting to compete with Nadia she was wearing very little make-up; a soft rose lipstick to match her dress, the merest hint of eyeshadow and mascara, and a soft blush of colour on her cheek bones.

The tea-rose perfume and body lotion she was wearing especially to complement her dress wafted delicately on the air when she walked, her waist in the rose satin dress small enough for Gavin to span with his hands when he measured it wonderingly. 'You'll be the belle of the ball,' he pronounced, 'just you wait and see.'

'I'm not planning to be,' Vanessa told him. 'I'm leaving that role to Nadia.'

Even though she knew she was looking her best, it was with a feeling of trepidation that she entered the hall of the manor half an hour later, grateful for the fact that Gavin was accompanying her.

New panelling adorned the walls, and Gavin murmured to her that it had once graced a house in the south of England which had recently been demolished. 'Jay thought it was in keeping with the stairs,' he added informatively. Vanessa glanced at them. The intricate carving was attributed to Grinling Gibbons and she had always admired it. Rich Persian rugs covered the parquet flooring, a huge floral decoration a brilliant splash of colour at the far end of the room.

As she had no coat to leave, Vanessa followed Gavin straight into the drawing room, accepting a glass of champagne from a passing waiter. The room was already full of people. Vanessa soon picked out several local dignatories, unaware of the interest she herself was attracting as she studied her surroundings.

'The main event is being held in the ballroom on the second floor,' Gavin told her. 'We'll make our way up there as soon as we can.' Vanessa could already hear the strains of waltz music reaching faintly from the upper room. She could also see Jeff with some other members of the team on the far side of the room and smiled at him warmly, pleased by the stunned surprise in his eyes when he recognised her.

'Ah, ha, here comes our host,' Gavin whispered, and Vanessa didn't care if he wondered why her fingers should suddenly grip his arm so tightly. Since her return from Spain Jay had never been mentioned between them except in connection with their work.

'Gavin.' Jay acknowledged her brother with a brief incline of his head. Nadia was clinging to his arm, and Vanessa's eyes widened fractionally as she took in the plunging neckline of her cousin's dress. The scarlet silk left little to the imagination and Vanessa could only applaud her cousin's sang-froid in wearing it. As she had suspected Nadia was heavily made up, her dark hair newly cut in a delicate feathering style that shaped her face.

'Vanessa, how frantically ante-bellum,' she murmured, hard sapphire eyes studying the rose taffeta dress, 'and frightfully débutante as well darling. A little young for you I would have said.'

'Vanessa.' Jay turned from Gavin to acknowledge her, no warmth in the gold glance as it slid impassively over her face. 'I must congratulate you on the shots you took of the team last week. They're really excellent.'

'Umm, wait until you hear the idea she's working on,' Gavin interrupted enthusiastically 'I'm sure you're going to like it.'

'Really?' Cold yellow eyes swept her dismissively. 'Then we'll have to talk about it some time.'

'Come on darling, I want to dance,' Nadia tugged impatiently on his arm, 'and Lord and Lady Carmichael are waiting to talk to you. Do come along.'

'Do you get the feeling we've just been well and truly put in our place?' Gavin asked ruefully as he took Vanessa's arm. 'Nadia is particularly nauseous when she's playing the Lady of the Manor.'

'Jay doesn't seem to think so.'

Somehow she managed to keep her voice even and blank, but Gavin wasn't deceived. 'I'm sorry Van,' he said softly. 'I really am. I like Jay, but I can't pretend to understand what he sees in Nadia.'

'Can't you?' Her voice was brittle. 'She's everything he wants, Gavin, and she doesn't tell lies.'

She was glad that Jeff came over to interrupt

them at that point and she and Gavin were both soon absorbed into a group of football players and their girlfriends and wives. At one o'clock when Vanessa subsided tiredly into one of the chairs in the ballroom, recovering from a particularly energetic polka, she eased off one of her shoes and studied the other dancers. Jay was dancing with Nadia, but she didn't look at them. It seemed to her that Jay had danced with every woman in the room apart from herself. Another underlining of his dislike of her. She ought to be getting accustomed to them by now, but she wasn't. All at once she wanted to go home. Her head ached, nearly as much as her feet, the gaiety of the other guests only serving to underline her own misery. It would be quite easy to slip away, Gavin was talking to the pretty daughter of the Mayor and wasn't likely to notice the disappearance of a mere sister. Jeff had already gone, pleading tiredness and the effects of intense training, so there was no one to dissuade her from going.

Downstairs in the hall, she was just walking past the library when a thought struck her. Tonight Gavin had broached the subject with Jay of the idea she had been working on, and Jay had said they could talk about it, but she knew that she would never be able to put it across to him without allowing her emotions to interfere with what she was trying to say, and that would undoubtedly prejudice his reaction. Her best bet was to write a brief outline of what she wanted to do, and to give him some of the photographs she had already done, to study. She had made notes of each one she had taken; the time; the event; the

reactions of the player when the shot was taken
and she was sure that they could all be built up to
give a detailed outline of a player's emotions
during the season; with the ups and downs
faithfully charted. She had taken shots of one
player playing a trombone; of another building a
model aircraft, including shots of families and
hobbies as well as ones of the game.

Thinking about her project helped to banish the
misery that engulfed her every time she saw Jay
with Nadia, and by the time she reached the lodge
she was deeply engrossed in her own private
thoughts. It only took a few minutes to gather
together her photographs, and half an hour more
to type out a brief outline of what she hoped to do
on Gavin's old portable machine. Armed with her
carefully arranged portfolio and the typed sheets
of paper, Vanessa headed back for the manor,
intending to leave them on Jay's desk in the
library, and then to slip home again, leaving them
for him to find in the morning.

As she drove back down the lane she had to
wait several times to make room for departing
cars; most of the guests seemed to be leaving and
there were only a handful of cars outside when she
parked the Volvo.

More guests were milling in the hall, saying their
goodbyes, so it was easy for her to slip into the
library and put the portfolio plus her outline on
Jay's desk. She hadn't been in the library since the
renovations and she lingered admiring the newly
installed bookshelves, glancing at the titles,
remembering the jumble of books in Jay's flat. The
same pattern was repeated here, classics mingling

with modern novels and textbooks. The original Georgian fireplace had been carefully restored, and over it hung a portrait of the late owner. She studied it sadly, wondering if Jay had felt bitter as he saw it hung, knowing that he would never be able to adorn the walls with portraits of his own ancestors. She was just stepping back from the empty grate when she heard the door open.

'Vanessa!' The door swung silently closed as Jay studied her. He had discarded his jacket and unfastened his tie, his shirt unbuttoned at the neck. He walked over to the desk and lifted the decanter resting on it, pouring a generous splash of brandy into a glass. 'I thought you'd left.'

'I had,' Vanessa agreed, wishing wildly that she had left before he came in, 'but I came back.'

'Am I allowed to ask why?'

His sardonic tone stung, colour seeped up under her pale skin. 'Not for any of the reasons you're imagining,' she said unwisely.

'Oh?' He dropped down into the chair behind the desk, swivelling it round and studying her so that she felt like a naughty junior summoned before the boss. 'Well then, leaving aside my imaginings, why are you here?'

'To leave this,' Vanessa told him, indicating the portfolio. 'The idea I had that Gavin was telling you about . . .'

'Couldn't it wait?' His eyebrows rose.

'Of course.' She managed to sound passably cool. 'But I wanted to give you the opportunity to study it before we discussed it. I thought this was the easiest way. I'd better go now,' she added uncertainly. 'Er. Where's Nadia?'

'Gone.' He stood up abruptly.

'Gone?'

'That's what I said.'

'But . . .'

'But you're still here, aren't you Vanessa. You're everywhere I look, do you know that? Haunting me with those sapphire eyes. Every time I see you they beg me to make love to you, do you know *that* Vanessa?'

'Jay. No . . . I . . .' She stumbled backwards as he walked towards her, panic clawing sharply through her stomach. There was something different about him tonight, something unleashed and dangerous.

Why had Nadia left him? Had they had a quarrel? Had her cousin grown bored? Vanessa had seen her dancing several times with a tall blond man. They had been laughing together, his arm wrapped round Nadia's waist.

'I won't be a substitute for Nadia, Jay,' she said wildly, 'I didn't come here for . . .'

'I know exactly what you came here for, and there's no question of you being a substitute for Nadia. Why are you looking at me like that?' he demanded harshly. 'I'm finally giving in, Vanessa; I'm finally going to do what you want. You do still want me to make love to you don't you?'

'No!' The sound was torn from her throat on a sob of anguish but he wasn't listening.

'No? Then why are you still a virgin? Why aren't you sleeping with Jeff Marsden? He wants you badly enough, you must know that, but you don't want him, do you, Vanessa? You want me.'

She closed her eyes, wanting to find the strength

to deny what he was saying, to tell him that he was
the last man on earth she wanted, but instead it
was a husky 'Yes,' that was drawn unwillingly
from her trembling lips, 'Damn you, yes,' she
blazed shakily, turning to bury her face in her
hands appalled by the intensity of that wanting.
With her back to him she didn't know Jay had
moved until she felt his arms lifting her. She
struggled against them.

'Jay . . .'

'Shut up Vanessa.' He said it thickly, his mouth
coming down on hers, hard and probing, stealing
her breath as well as her reason.

When he lifted his head, Jay's eyes were glowing
hotly. 'Tonight I'm going to make love to you,' he
said slowly and without another word he carried
her out of the room and through the now deserted
hall.

Like someone in a dream Vanessa voiced no
protest, clinging to the broad outline of his
shoulders, closing her eyes as he climbed the stairs,
and not opening then again until she felt him
lowering her slowly to the floor, his hands locked
round her waist.

'You wanted me to make love to you, tonight
I'm going to.' Her face was on a level with his, his
hands still gripping her waist.

'Jay . . .'

'No words, Vanessa, no words.' His tongue
stroked her tremulous mouth, the twin crescents of
his lashes fanning his olive cheeks as his eyes
closed in sensual appreciation of his self-imposed
task. Something flickered to life inside her, a wild
hungry need that leapt to meet the subtle mastery

of his touch. Her lips parted, his tongue running quickly along the vulnerable inner smoothness, his teeth tugging impatiently at her bottom lip. 'Kiss me back Vanessa.' He breathed the command into her mouth. 'I know you want to.'

CHAPTER TEN

AFTER that she was lost. There was no gradual giving in to the seductive pull of her own senses; it was more like going straight over the top of a cliff. One moment she was secure on firm ground the next she wasn't. Jay had no need to urge her lips to cling yearningly to his, they were doing it of their own accord, her teeth nipping urgently at the full curve of his lower lip, her tongue running lightly over the upper one, her body melting against his.

'Vanessa!' He moaned her name into her mouth, reaching for the zip at the back of her dress, the rustle of the silk taffeta as it fell to the floor at her feet a seductive accompaniment to the soft words of encouragement he was murmuring against her skin.

His lips left her throat to return to hers, his hands sliding down her body moulding her against him and she was utterly and completely lost, giving in to the wild tug of desire beating through her. All she wanted was here within her grasp, her only desire to share with the man holding her in his arms the complete union her own body craved.

'Vanessa, love me.' It was the cry of a small child muffled against her throat; a plea from the lonely boy he must once have been, piercingly bitter-sweet, even though she knew it translated as 'Vanessa, make love to me'. Whatever its meaning it was enough to destroy the barriers she had tried to erect against him. Her hands found their way inside his shirt, loving the sensation of his skin beneath them.

She bent her head, touching her lips to the ridged muscles of his throat, tracing their movements as he swallowed back a fierce groan, his fingers wrenching the supporting pins out of her hair as he bent his head and buried his face in its scented silkiness. And then he was tilting her head back, kissing her with a hunger he had never exhibited before, fierce, hungry kisses that drained and dizzied her, interspersed with muttered words of praise and demand. 'Kiss me, Vanessa.' He shuddered as she complied, her lips exploring the taut column of his throat. 'Touch me.' Her hands spread out against the damp warmth of his chest, stroking the heated skin until he shivered and muttered something into her hair, his fingers caressing the outline of her spine until she arched into him under the stimulus of the tormenting caress, her arms locking round him.

'I want to look at you—all of you.' She unlocked her arms reluctantly, as he pushed her lightly away from him, suddenly shy as he studied the naked outline of her breasts in the dim glow of the lamplit bedroom. And then before she had time to register any protest, he dropped to the floor in front of her, half kneeling as he balanced himself, his movements deft but gentle as he removed the rest of her clothes, lightly kissing the inside of her thigh, his fingers tensing over her hip as he felt the unmistakable shudder of response that racked through her.

'You like that?' His voice sounded thick and slurred his mouth returning to her silky quivering skin. Her finger nails dug protestingly into his shoulder, her body swaying as she fought to control the intensity of her response. She wanted to cry out with the pleasure of it, to slide her fingers into the night darkness of his hair and hold him against her. 'Yes, yes I know.' His voice was hoarse, his teeth nipping delicately at her soft skin in response to the pressure of her nails against his spine. He stood up, lifting her against him as he had done before, but this time there was not the barrier of her dress between them. Her hands clung to his shoulders beneath his shirt, as she looked down at him, shivering uncontrollably as his hands spanned her waist and he began to tease brief kisses in a line downwards from where the pulse thudded eratically at the base of her throat to the valley between her breasts.

She felt Jay shudder as she arched into him, moaning softly, unable to control her fevered response, tiny gasping cries of pleasure drawn from deep inside her as his tongue circled the pink hardness of each nipple and then caressed them until she was burning with feverish urgency, a yielding molten tide pouring through her veins.

'Jay, love me, please love me.'

She was barely aware of crying out the words until she heard him respond thickly, 'I'm going to. All night long. You can't know how my body's ached for you.' He carried her over to the bed and shrugged off his shirt. His hands were on his belt when she sat up, her eyes glittering febrilely as she moved towards him taking over his task. His own hands dropped away as he allowed her to complete it for him and then returned to stroke over her shoulders, cupping her breasts.

Beneath the dark fabric of his trousers he was wearing equally dark briefs. Vanessa's fingers curled nervelessly against the dark material, unable to continue their task. She could feel the tension in Jay's body; his arousal impossible to hide as he moved impatiently against her muttering thickly. 'I want to feel all of you against me Vanessa. All of you against all of me without anything between us.' One hand left her breast while the other continued to cradle and caress the soft swell of her flesh, his free hand imprisoning hers against his body, uncurling her fingers, urging them against him as he shed the last of his clothing. Wonderingly she touched the vibrant masculinity of his body, sharing the shudder that racked him, gasping aloud with mingled pain and pleasure as he bent his head to capture the aching tip of her breast in his teeth, tugging gently, and then releasing her to mutter rawly against her swollen breast. 'You taste so good Vanessa, so sweet and warm that I can't seem to get enough of you.'

His tongue stroked across her nipple and she shivered violently resting her head against his hip, weak with longing and love, her mouth warmly moist as she pressed desperate kisses against his skin. She heard him groan and felt his fingers wind into her hair as his body tensed against her. 'Touch me like that again, and I won't be responsible for what happens next.'

It was a warning she was powerless to heed. Her

lips and hands seemed to have developed a will of
their own, exploring and tasting the taut male
body with increasing intimacy, fuelled by a hunger
that Jay incited with his soft shudders of pleasure
and the harsh sounds he stifled in his throat, until
at last he stopped trying to urge her away from
him and instead wrapped his arms tightly round
her, letting his body dictate his responses to her
feverish caresses.

'Vanessa!' She felt the bite of his fingers in her
soft flesh as he grasped her beneath the arms,
lifting her in a movement that brought him on to
the bed beside her, his mouth finding hers in a kiss
of blind need that stole her breath and left her
clinging helplessly to his shoulders.

'Now it's my turn to torment you.' He pushed
her on to her back stroking his hand down her
body until it found the curve of her hip. It stayed
there holding her down against the bed while his
mouth trailed light kisses along her collar bone
and then down. She closed her eyes, a victim of the
deep heat burning inside her, caressing the smooth
shape of his back, shivering as his breath grazed
her too responsive skin. 'I want to taste each bit of
you, all of you.' His tongue flicked lightly against
her nipple and she arched wildly beneath him, the
hot mutter of satisfaction he gave when his mouth
closed over her burning flesh echoing the silent
scream of need she had been suppressing. 'You feel
so good.' He looked up at her, his eyes a blazing
topaz ringed with fire. 'So very good.' His mouth
closed over her breast as though he couldn't resist
the taste of it, his hand releasing her hip to stroke
the quivering softness of her stomach. Her body

arched compulsively and his hand moved, his
fingers deft as they stroked and aroused, teaching
her things she hadn't known about her own body;
eliciting a fevered response that seemed to send her
beyond the realms of sanity to a place where there
was only sensation, and a tight coiling need
building up inside her that screamed to be
released. She felt Jay move, the hard arousal of his
body against hers, his fingers stroking, soothing,
and then compellingly urgent.

'Jay, please.' The words seemed to burst from
her throat, her teeth biting into the firm skin of his
shoulder.

'Vanessa.' She felt the shudder rip through him.
'I don't want to hurt you, but . . .' He muttered
something under his breath, resting his forehead
against her briefly. It was damp with his sweat and
as he breathed deeply against her she could smell
the musky fragrance of his body.

'Vanessa.' He kissed her lightly, his mouth
moving over hers, gradually deepening the kiss
until she was lost under it, barely aware of the
weight of him between her thighs until he moved
against her and she felt her body tense with the
onset of panic.

'Shush.' His mouth brushed her eyes and she felt
him lift and thrust himself against her. 'Open your
eyes, there's nothing to be afraid of. You wanted
this, remember?'

Her eyes were squeezed tightly closed but she
opened them looking reluctantly into his. They
still glowed molten gold but it was a steady glow
that reassured her. 'Now look. Watch.' His
mouth brushed her cheek and then her lips, his

hand cupping her jaw forcing her to look down the length of their joined bodies. 'There's nothing to be afraid of.' He moved, gently and she watched in fascination, her panic forgotten. Sweat clung damply to his chest darkening the crisp whorls of hair. She raised her hand to smooth the tangled darkness and gasped as she felt the sudden brief pain and the urgency that came with it, the fear of the unknown suddenly leaving her muscles to be replaced by an aching tension that made her cry out and arch upwards instinctively the brief sound stifled by Jay's mouth as it opened over hers, his arms locking her against his body as it tutored hers to match the rhythm of his possession.

A fierce heat licked through her veins, her fingers stroking feverishly down his back, finding the flat, masculine buttocks, losing herself completely in the storm of pleasure Jay was invoking, crying out in astonished pleasure when she felt the universe explode around her, hearing Jay moan her name with harsh satisfaction. The last sound she remembered as she slid down into the deep darkness of a completely relaxed sleep.

Something was wrong, but she couldn't imagine what it was. She could never remember experiencing such a sense of physical wellbeing, but something nagged at the corner of her mind, worming its way into her sleep of satisfaction, ordering her to think. She moved, blinking as she turned away from the bright sunlight dancing red against her closed eyes. That was what was wrong, the morning sun didn't shine into her bedroom.

She opened her eyes and stared at the unfamiliar room.

'Good morning.'

Her head lifted, her eyes finding the masculine figure standing by the door. 'Jay.' He was carrying a tray of tea and toast.

'I thought you might be hungry.' He said it blandly enough but hot colour stormed her face as her mind forced her to confront the various meanings that might be hidden within the surface innocuousness of his statement.

'I . . .' She started to sit up and then changed her mind, realising that she had nothing on, and then realising the foolishness of adopting a modest pose now. No wonder Jay was laughing at her.

'Happy now?' he drawled quizzically, strolling over to the bed, and putting the tray on the table beside her, before he perched on the edge of the bed. He had an unfair advantage Vanessa decided bitterly, not only was he dressed, he also had years of experience of this sort of thing behind him, whereas she . . .

'I'd like to get up and get dressed,' she said primly avoiding the question. 'What time is it?'

Jay glanced at the gold watch strapped to his wrist. Strange how such a small gesture should have the power to turn her stomach to melting weakness. 'Just gone ten. I'll go down and collect some clothes for you. Anything you want in particular?'

'I . . .' To her mortification dark colour seeped under her skin. How casual he sounded, whereas she . . .

'Having second thoughts?' Don't you think it's

rather late for those now? You wanted what happened last night, Vanessa, no matter how much you might want to deny it now.' He had withdrawn from her, his eyes no longer teasing but cold.

'I . . .'

'Eat your breakfast, I'll go down to the lodge. I won't be long. When I come back we'll talk.'

'Jay, it isn't necessary . . . I . . .'

'You what? Jump in and out of bed with every man who takes your fancy? We both know that isn't true, Vanessa. You may not think the fact that you wanted me to be your first lover is worthy of discussion but I happen to think differently. For one thing . . . Eat your breakfast,' he commanded her. 'We'll talk when I come back.'

She didn't hear the sound of the Ferrari, so she guessed that he must have walked. What on earth must Gavin be thinking? She shivered remembering the events of the night, colour stinging her face in painful bursts. How could she have been so abandoned? Quite easily a small voice mocked her, it was easy for any woman to be abandoned with the man she loved, especially when he was the expert lover that Jay was.

She heard the car just as she was pouring her second cup of tea, and frowned as she heard the front door slam, and then footsteps heading for the bedroom. The door was flung open with impatient haste.

'Jay it's me, Nadia.' Vanessa heard her cousin call out as she stepped inside. 'I'm sorry about last night but . . .' Nadia froze as she saw the slim figure hunched in the bed.

'You,' she hissed venomously. 'Well, well, I suppose I should have guessed. You're playing substitute again are you? Well this time I've no doubt that Jay noticed the difference. Jay likes his women experienced and sensual darling, hardly adjectives anyone would apply to you. I know why you're here of course. Jay did it to pay me out for our quarrel, but once he knows I'm ready to make up, he'll throw you out so quickly that you won't know what's hit you. What's the matter darling,' Nadia cooed viciously, 'did you think you'd got him for keeps?' She laughed, her eyes glittering with savage dislike. 'Jay's mine Vanessa, and I hope you enjoyed what you had with him last night, because it's all you're going to get. Jay and I quarrelled because he was being stupidly jealous over Ben, and I decided to teach him a lesson. Do you think he'll want *you* when he knows I've come back? Would any man prefer *you* to me.' She advanced to the bed, wrenching back the covers before Vanessa could stop her, her eyes darkening to near fury as she saw the tell tale bruises on the pale flesh; the marks of Jay's lovemaking branded into her skin.

'Nadia!' Neither of them had heard Jay come in. Nadia spun round at the sound of his voice, and Vanessa grabbed back the covers, yanking them protectively around her.

'Darling, how could you do this to us?' Nadia demanded reproachfully. She crossed the room and flung herself into his arms. Vanessa closed her eyes unable to watch any more.

'We'll talk downstairs,' she heard Jay saying to her cousin. 'Vanessa, here are your clothes.' His voice sounded clipped and cold, and no wonder. No doubt he had hoped to have her out of the house and out of his life before Nadia came back. So he used you because he couldn't have Nadia, didn't you know that all the time, a tiny voice goaded, but nothing could stop the pain, nothing at all. Not the icy sting of the shower as she tried to wash his touch off her body nor the tears that ran helplessly from her eyes as she stood under the savage onslaught of water. Nothing. At last, too exhausted to stand the cold lash of the shower any longer, she stepped out wrapping herself in a thick towel, her teeth chattering from a mixture of self-inflicted pain and misery. The sooner she was dressed and away from here the better, she told herself. In fact the sooner she left Clarewell altogether the better. She couldn't stay now. She would have to leave.

As she opened the bathroom door she heard the roar of a car engine. Nadia and Jay leaving, hopefully. No doubt having made up their quarrel they were giving her time to quit the house without any further awkward scenes. Well that suited her. There was no way she was able to face the sight of her cousin locked in the same arms that had held her so tightly last night, right at this moment. She stepped into the bedroom, coming to an abrupt halt as she saw Jay locking the bedroom door and pocketing the key.

'That should ensure at least that we don't have any more interruptions,' he said grimly, frowning as he saw her teeth chattering.

'What's the matter with you?' He reached her in two strides, taking in the fall of wet hair and the pinched look of her skin. He reached out, brushing her cheek with his fingers, his eyes darkening to livid gold as she flinched away. 'Damn you, Vanessa, I'm not going to *hurt* you,' he said thickly. 'Just what kind of man do you think I am?'

'The kind who makes love to one woman because she's a substitute for another,' Vanessa said bitterly.

'And you'd condemn me for that?'

She looked at him incredulously. 'Do you mean you think I shouldn't?'

'I can understand what you must feel, but try to see my point of view. I tried to be honest with you right from the start. You knew I thought you were Nadia.'

'But I thought you wanted *me*,' Vanessa told him fiercely. 'I knew who you thought I was, but I thought you wanted me.'

'You knew how I felt about permanent commitments. Surely you knew I'd fight against anything like that. Is it so hard to understand?'

'*That* isn't hard to understand,' she agreed tonelessly, turning her back to him and tensing into the protection of her bathsheet, 'but it makes me feel physically sick to know that you would use a woman simply to appease a sexual appetite. You knew how I felt about you . . .'

'And that was supposed to make it easier?' His face was contorted with fury. 'Damn you Vanessa, how the hell do you think I felt, knowing you loved me; knowing you wanted me; knowing how much I damned well ached for you and yet telling myself that I couldn't have you, because I couldn't give you the commitment you wanted? All right, so I used your cousin, do you think she's never pulled the same stunt? Do you think she's loved every man she's been to bed with?' He shook his head. 'Do you think I could have made love to you the way I did last night if I was getting everything I needed from Nadia? Oh she's very skilful, I'll admit,' he agreed sardonically, 'but all of Nadia's skill couldn't arouse me as much as a simple look from you. All right, so when I held her in my arms I pretended she was you. Okay, so last night I told her it was all over between us. I thought you'd be pleased, not ranting and raving at me as though I'd broken the heart of your best friend. If the positions were reversed do you think she'd spare you so much as a single tear? Do you?' he grated, suddenly reaching for her and shaking her, the violence leaving him as quickly as it had come as he bent his head and licked an errant drop of moisture from her pale skin. 'I wanted to shower with you this morning,' he told her rawly, 'I wanted to touch your skin, to feel you come to life beneath my hands the way you did last night, and then to make love to you with no restraints between us. I've tried to fight it ... I've tried to pretend it's just desire; but none of it works.'

'Jay ...' He saw the bewilderment in her eyes and released her 'Don't read me any more lectures about substituting your cousin for you Vanessa,' he said harshly. 'I've already learned my lesson. "Gold and dross" I once called the pair of you, only I got the descriptions the wrong way round and I think I knew it then, but I fought against it. I didn't want to want you, damn you, I wanted the shallow, self glorifying woman I knew your cousin to be because I knew I'd be safe with her, no commitment, no danger of giving something of myself to someone who might leave me and hurt me, who might not love me, even though everything about her told me that she did.'

'You wanted *me*?' Her legs were trembling so much she had to sit down on the edge of the bed.

'You really need to ask that after last night?' He sounded grimly incredulous and she looked at him frowning slightly.

'You and Nadia were lovers, I had nothing . . . no way of comparing . . . I thought . . . and then this morning when Nadia came here and told me that you were just using me because you and she had quarrelled and she'd left you . . .'

'Left me?' He laughed harshly. 'The boot was very much on the other foot. Your cousin had let it be known that she wanted to make our very casual relationship extremely permanent, and I had told her no way. I also told her there was only one woman I could marry; only one woman I could love,' he added throatily, reaching out to caress the curve of her cheekbone and jaw.

'But you made love to her.'

'Briefly, and somewhat unsuccessfully. It was very hard to keep the sweetness of your image in my mind when I looked into the hardness of Nadia's eyes. Is that why you were so furious with me just now? Because you thought I'd been substituting you for Nadia?'

'What else *was* I to think? You'd already made it plain which one of us you preferred.'

'Had I?' He eyed her broodingly.

'Nadia thought . . .'

'Nadia knew last night that I loved you. I was fully intending to come and see you this morning to talk to you. When I walked into the library last night and found you there it seemed like the God given answer to all my prayers. So much had gone wrong between us. I'd wanted you so badly and yet been unable to admit to myself that I loved you. I seized on the excuse of saying I preferred Nadia, even though I knew it wasn't true. I was frightened you see, terrified of committing myself to another person. I told myself you looked so alike that it wouldn't make any difference; that I could satisfy my hunger for you with Nadia, but I knew the first time I kissed her just how different you really are. There's no comparison,' he said softly brushing his lips across her half parted mouth. 'No comparison at all. I nearly went crazy when you were in Spain. I half expected you to take a lover while you were there. I even hoped you would because it would prove that I had been right all along; that all women are the same under the skin, but you didn't. And then there was Marsden.

'The night I saw you coming out of his room was the worst of my life. When you told me you hadn't made love I felt so primitively pleased, but I still couldn't bring myself to admit the truth.'

'And that is?'

'That I'm madly, crazily in love with you and that without you my life is completely meaningless. Even worse, I'm not going to let you leave this house until you promise you're going to marry me. You see,' he said whimsically, 'it's the old story of the reformed rake. Now that I've seen the light, I'm determined to make you see it as well. I know I've hurt you Vanessa, I can't even pretend that it wasn't deliberate, but I had to hold you at an arm's length and because I wasn't strong enough to do it myself I had to use you to do it for me. Because of the lessons I learned early on in my life I swore I'd never let anyone get close enough to me to hurt me, but I was wrong Vanessa; there are worse things than being hurt by the people we love. There's not having love at all; not ever. The nights I've lain in that bed, dreaming of the silken warmth of you, dreaming of losing myself in you, of being part of you. You can't know how I've yearned for that completeness; and how I've fought against wanting it. Can you forgive me?'

So easily that it was frightening. She knew instinctively now that he was telling her the truth; that she had always been the one he wanted, and that his own sense of what he felt to be right had not allowed him simply to seduce her, knowing how she felt about him.

This was confirmed when he came to her, pulling her into his arms murmuring. 'That very first time I held you, I already knew, but I denied it to myself, telling myself you were no different from all the rest. I thought I was on safe ground; that you were just another game player like myself, and when I discovered the truth I also discovered how dangerously I'd broken my self-imposed rules. That's why I was so angry and why I blamed you. I told myself you had cheated me by pretending to be someone else, even though I knew it was you I wanted ... whatever name you chose to adopt.'